Also by Frank Moorhouse

FORTY–SEVENTEEN

• FORTY–SEVENTEEN •

FRANK MOORHOUSE

First published in Australia in 1988
by Viking Penguin Books Australia Ltd
Ringwood, Victoria 3134
First published in Great Britain in 1988
by Faber and Faber Limited
3 Queen Square London WCIN 3AU

Printed in Australia
by Australian Print Group, Maryborough, Victoria.

© Frank Moorhouse, 1988

British Library Cataloguing in Publication Data

Moorhouse Frank, *1938-*
Forty-seventeen.
I. Title
823 [F]

ISBN 0-571-15210-4

• CONTENTS •

• BUENAVENTURA DURRUTI'S •
FUNERAL

The American poet's visit.   After lunch over coffee and stregas at Sandro's the poets showed their pens. Two of the poets had Lamys, another a pen from the New York Museum of Modern Art which looked like a scalpel . A fifth said he thought he'd 'get a Lamy'.

They handled each other's pens, writing their favourite line from Yeats or Eliot or whoever. 'Mere anarchy is loosed upon the world, one wrote. He had not seen poets at this before.

He then made a reluctant presentation of a book of Australian stories to the visiting American poet Philip Levine, for whom the lunch had been organised. He said the book contained the story *The American Poet's Visit* and that he had been induced to present it by his friends as a 'joke *Australien*'.

'Did Rexroth ever read the story?' Levine asked, after being told that it was about the American poet Kenneth Rexroth.

This wasn't known.

When we here, he gestured at the table, were all younger, Australians wrote with a perspective which came from feeling that we lived outside the 'real world'. For us, Europe and the US were the world. We lived somewhere else.

1

Australians wrote with the greatest freedom there is – writing without fear of being read.

He observed to himself that the others at the table had made it as writers while he'd gone other ways. Though he had tried it for a time.

'That's right,' said John, 'without the fear of being read by anyone really.'

A joke for John, a bitter truth for him.

'Further, people from the real world were, paradoxically, people from literary history and they had a fictional gloss to them – you were not of the world of *Meanjin*.'

'*Meanjin?*' asked Levine.

'Our literary world, I mean.'

'It's the Aboriginal word meaning "rejected from the *New Yorker*",' someone else said.

Levine, or someone at the table, said that now someone else would be able to write another story – *The Second American Poet's Visit*.

'Ah there cannot be another story because we are being read now by the people from "out there".'

Everyone fell thoughtfully glum at this observation.

'But when the first story was published the editor thought "Rexroth" was a pseudonym for a "real person".'

'And Philip isn't the second poet to visit, there's been Duncan, Ginsberg, Simpson.'

'Kinnel, Levertov, Snyder.'

'Strand.'

'The Harlem Globe Trotters.'

'We are now part of the poetry night–club circuit.'

'The poets arrive – we look them up in Norton's *Anthology of Modern American Verse* so that we can quote them a line or two of their poetry.'

'Speak for yourself,' said John.

In this cafe, Durruti,
the Unnameable
Plotted the burning of the bishop of Saragossa.

'Very good,' said Levine, 'they are indeed my lines from Norton's.'

Levine said that although Norton's was laboriously footnoted for students there was no footnote for his poem *The Midget* to explain who 'Durruti' was or the 'Archbishop of Saragossa'.

'Do you people know?'

We shook our heads expectantly.

He wrote down the name Durruti and the name Archbishop of Saragossa on a table napkin because of the noise in the restaurant and we passed it around, reading the names.

A biography of Durruti is reviewed in the TLS. He wrote to his friend Cam Perry in Montreal, a professor of hypnosis, and asked him to get the biography of Durruti which was published in Montreal by Black Rose Books and reviewed in the *Times Literary Supplement*.

He said in the letter to Cam, 'By the way, my friend Belle says that because I work for the UN I can't be really decadent. I didn't spend all that money at night clubs and go through all those squalid situations when we were young to be told that I'm not decadent. You were there – write to her . . . ' He wrote jokingly to Levine, now back in California, saying that there was a biography of Durruti and that Norton should be informed so that they could make a footnote in the anthology.

The Archbishop. The Archbishop of Saragossa was shot dead in 1923 as an anarchist act – 'a cleansing social act'. He was a key figure in the repression of that city. Popular rumour said that he held weekly orgies at a convent which in itself seemed to be something of a redeeming feature of the Archbishop. When he died he left his fortune to a nun who then deserted her order.

At the time of the shooting Durruti and the Los Solidarios (an anarchist commando group) were blamed – 'credited'? – and while they almost certainly planned the execution, the actual shooting was probably done by Francisco Ascaso, a close friend of Durruti. But it was said that Ascaso was the stone, Durruti the blade.

In Sydney we always said assassination was ultimate censorship. But things were tougher in Saragossa.

Durruti lived in Barcelona. Barcelona he knew visually from Michelangelo Antonioni's film *The Passenger* and Luis Buñuel's film *That Obscure Object of Desire*, and he knew about the Barcelona telephone exchange and Durruti from his reading about the Spanish Civil War. There'd been no real point in telling Levine or the poets that he did know who Durruti was.

In 1936 Durruti and the anarchists gained control of the Barcelona Telefonica and collectivised it. The communists at this time were plotting to destroy the power of the anarchists and the battle for the exchange was part of this power struggle. When calls came to Barcelona for 'the government' the anarchist operators would instruct the caller in anarchist theory and tell them there was no 'government' recognised by the anarchists in Barcelona. Although it slowed down telephone calls the control of the exchange was useful as a 'school' for the anarchists and their callers. And it should be mentioned that, the Telefonica aside, most functions run by the anarchists were well run.

The Passenger was a special film for him. *The Passenger* is about a journalist (played by Jack Nicholson) who is approaching forty and who takes on the identity of a casual acquaintance after the acquaintance dies while they are together in a hotel in North Africa. Nicholson lives out the man's life and appointments.

It is in Barcelona that Nicholson meets a young student – Maria Schneider – who involves herself with him on his drive along the Spanish coast from Barcelona through Armeria, Purellana, and Algeciras. He keeps the final appointment in the Hotel de la Gloria and meets the other man's destiny – he is shot dead in that hotel.

The film was special for him because he'd been approaching forty when he'd met a seventeen–year–old school girl in Adelaide – he'd been there visiting the weapons testing facility. On erotic impulse he had asked her to drive with him to Darwin – 5000 kilometres clean across the continent and back again. She had said without hesitation, 'Yes.'

'Your mother?'

'She'll be OK.'

They had driven the first 1000 kilometres at 160–80 kilometres an hour hardly speaking, just observation and occasional biographical anecdote, straight across the desert and made love at the small town of Arkaroola in a motel which had not yet been cleaned by the staff but they could not wait.

She had been transfixingly erotic for him and the silent interplay was intricate – uniquely so and he'd told her this. She took the compliment and said gracefully, 'My body is young but I know some things about its pleasures'. She said she thought she understood 'sexual mood'.

On that drive across the first 1000 kilometres before they'd made love his desire for her had grown unbearable and he had stopped the car out in the desert and suggested they walk for a little, with the intention of making physical contact with her.

They'd stood there in the desert. He had moved to kiss her but received no signal of permission.

'Look,' he'd said, 'I can't take this uncertainty, my body, my heart can't take it – you will make love with me when we reach the next town?'

'Of course I will,' she'd said, 'let's go,' and then moved back to the car before he could take her in his arms. He'd felt the pact should have been sealed affectionately. But then he'd thought that maybe she did not go in for the 'affectionate sealing of pacts'.

In the motel they had not drunk alcohol, which was unusual for him but he'd felt no need. After their first lovemaking she'd come to him and coaxed him back into her saying, 'Give me more,' and he'd had no trouble making love to her again.

Despite the intricacy of their silent interplay she'd had difficulty talking to him at times and he had had to 'make' the conversation.

Though during the drive across the desert, before the lovemaking but after the pact, she had turned to him and asked, teasingly, 'Do you find me very young?'

'Yes,' he said smiling, 'do you find me very much older?'

'Yes and I like it.'

'So do I.'

In Darwin he'd found a copy of Turgenev's *First Love*.

'In this book,' he said, 'the father competes with the son for the love of a girl.'

'Who wins?'

'The father. It is a book which you read first from the son's point of view and then later in life you read it from the father's point of view. A male does. I don't know how it reads from a female point of view.'

'I'll tell you,' she said.

A year later she said, 'You know you gave me Turgenev's *First Love* to read and you said you didn't know how it read from "a female point of view"?'

He said, yes, he remembered.

'Well,' she said, 'it reads acceptably well from this female's point of view,' and she laughed, half privately, and he guessed he was being compared with her young boyfriend.

He had continued to see her in the years that followed, during her vacations from university, and they'd meet in motels somewhere in

Australia. They had other long drives in different places in three states. He had not been shot in any hotels. Inevitably he would be at the motel first, awaiting her. She would arrive with her tube tote, which she called her 'parachute bag', stuffed with a few things and many books which would never be opened during the trip.

They would always refer to *The Passenger* and recall favourite details.

He had during one of their trips talked to her about a possible journey to Spain as a homage to the Spanish anarchists and to *The Passenger* and to Buñuel.

She had laughingly refused to take the idea of a pilgrimage to Spain seriously. 'Why should I know anything about the Spanish Civil War – except to know who were good and who were bad?' He did not know whether it was because she thought the pilgrimage unlikely or whether she didn't want to be too much a part of his fantasies.

'There are the "real" lessons of the Spanish Civil War,' he said, but she did not pick up the question and he refrained from overloading her with his preoccupations.

He on the other hand had taken the pilgrimage too seriously. He said to her a few times that they would do it the year he turned forty and she graduated.

He listed the places they would visit. Madrid University which the Durruti Column had defended and near where Durruti had been shot, the Ritz Hotel where he had been taken to die, the Hotel Victoria in Valencia where Auden and the others drank. The Hotel Gaylord in Madrid from *For Whom the Bell Tolls*. The Hotel Continental where Orwell stayed during the war. The Hotel Christian where Hemingway's *Fifth Column* is set.

'And the Ritz in Madrid is one of the twenty leading hotels of the world.'

But she would stop the conversation before it got too far.

In a motel dining room in some Victorian coastal town one night she said, 'But if we did that you'd be shot in a hotel room like Jack.'

'Do you really think that?' He took her hand.

And then a darkness passed over her face and she said she did not wish to talk about it, as if she had forebodings.

Hypnotic coercion and compliance to it.   Instead of the biography of Durruti, Cam sent him a copy of one of his academic papers published in the *International Journal of Clinical and Experimental*

Hypnosis. It was about the potential of hypnosis to coerce unconsenting behaviour. One position asserts that coercion is possible through the induction of distorted perceptions which delude the hypnotised person into believing that the behaviour is not transgressive. The other position asserts that where hypnosis appears to be a causal factor in coercing behaviour, the other elements in the situation, especially a close hypnotist–client relationship, were probably the main determinants of behaviour.

He read the paper with delight from the things people did with their lives and from the way these things entered his life.

Cam said the Durruti book would follow.

Up at the Journalists' Club.   Up at the Journalists' Club he and his ex-wife Robyn met some old friends from his cadetship days and following a joke about the anarchists/and the Barcelona telephone exchange – a joke they'd been enjoying since those days – they argued over what was the last battle fought in the Spanish Civil War.

He said he was more interested in the 'real' lessons of the Spanish Civil War.

'The Spanish Civil War is not behind us,' he said suddenly, 'it is in front of us.'

'The bitch is on heat again,' Barry said.

'No.' he said, 'I mean that it is not the war with the fascists which is ahead of us but the war between the free left and the authoritarian left.'

'Poland,' said Tony.

'The real lesson of the Spanish Civil War is that in this country not everyone who calls themselves Left is Left.'

'We still have to break the haughty power of capital,' Barry said.

'We are breaking capital's haughty power.'

'Oh yeah?'

Tony said that Durruti was nothing more than a pistolero.

' "The anarchists were generous but they were still political gangsters",' quoted Barry.

'*Obscure Object of Desire,*' he and Tony answered simultaneously.

'Correct,' said Barry, 'I think Tony was a fraction faster.'

'There was the defence of the University of Madrid.'

'Durruti's Column fled – proving the fundamental unreliability of anarchist formations,' said Tony.

'But they were the last days of Simple Anarchism,' Barry said wistfully.

'What of the moral bigotry of anarchism – their unpalatable behaviour towards homosexuals and prostitutes,' said Tony.

'Admitted,' said Barry.

'Sydney Anarchism eradicated moralism and replaced it with Higher Libertarianism.'

'Of course.' They all laughed.

'Go to the communes for moral bigotry.'

'I am still a Friend of Durruti,' he said.

'I can't believe this,' Robyn said 'Am I in the Journalists' Club in Sydney and hearing this? I can't believe this conversation. No. Yes, I can.'

We all laughed hard with her, some of us knew she was dying of cancer.

'Durruti was the front man of anarchism in Spain but it was Ascaso who was the theoretician. I am a friend of Ascaso,' said Tony.

'Let us drink to the discipline of indiscipline which must guide us all in every action,' he said.

'Pinch me, am I dreaming?' said Robyn.

'I drink to Cantwell who was an anarchist shot by the Viet Cong.'

'An anarchist who worked for *Time*.'

'There are many anarchist traditions.'

Later he said to Barry that he had never quite understood all the ramifications of the 'discipline of indiscipline'.

'There is much to be said on that subject,' Barry said but did not elaborate.

The tide is high.   He received a letter from her saying that in her final vacation she was working with the Elcho Island Aboriginal Crafts centre. 'I have been thinking of you big mobs – as they say up here – and the tide is high, as Deborah Harry says, and I have a feeling that it is getting close to that trip to Spain you talked so much and so often about. And you'll be turning forty soon. I'm planning my Grand Tour now that I'm nearly finished.'

He was deeply pleased that she had raised the trip to Spain. He wrote to her asking who was Deborah Harry?

He joined her on Elcho Island and they fished for parrot fish and speared mud crabs and cooked on hot coals.

In a motel in her home city after their return they'd made love. She had said that she had to go soon because her boyfriend was waiting. She had looked at him with her childlike eyes and said, 'Will you want me again before I go?'

'Yes, I will – now that you have asked me – it was the asking which aroused me.'

'I thought it would arouse you.' she said, smiling knowingly.

Searching for Durruti.   He wrote to Levine in California.

I'm planning a pilgrimage to the Spanish Civil War and would like to include the anarchist pilgrimage. My own guess is that your poem 'The Midget' is set in a cafe that 'could have been' the cafe in which Durruti plotted? Or is it a well known cafe? (I guess I sound like an MA student).

A curious day.   He wrote to her.

It looks as if our Spanish pilgrimage may then be shaping up. I had a curious day. I am writing again. Trying. I was working on the Buenaventura Durruti story (which is dedicated to you), my first story for years. It is a long way from finished but it is a collection of references to Durruti, Barcelona, *The Passenger* and you. Last night I (and my ex-wife Robyn) met some old mates from my cadetship days at the Journalists' Club and we argued about the Spanish Civil War – today your letter came saying that you might be ready to go to Spain with me. It would fit in with the General Conference of the IAEA* and side business I have in Vienna and other places. I did not think you ever took the trip to Spain seriously . . .

The discipline of indiscipline (I).   The next week in the *New York Review of Books* he read a reference to the problems of Durruti and the discipline of indiscipline. Bernard Knox, who had been in the International Brigade, said,

Madrid in the winter of 1936–7 was a remarkable place. The word epic has often been used of the events of that time but there was also a surrealist quality to it. I have often thought since that Luis Buñuel, if he had been there, would have felt quite at home.

*The International Atomic Energy Agency which supervises the international use of nuclear fuel and the non-proliferation treaty.

Knox said that Durruti created the idea of a 'discipline of indiscipline'. He had once talked with the Durruti Column to discuss passwords and patrol routes. Knox said he was plied with cigars, chorizo sausage and wine:

needless to say the passwords we had arranged were quickly forgotten and they fired on our supply column that night . . . and when Durruti led his men back into the line he was shot dead and the Column disintegrated . . . the Anarchist columns . . . had shown almost superhuman courage in the fight in Barcelona but facing experienced troops in the field they were soon outmanoeuvered and outflanked whereupon they ran like rabbits . . .

William Herrick took issue in the next *New York Review of Books*. 'There isn't a fighting force on earth whether communist, anarchist, fascist or whatever that has not at one point or another run like rabbits.'
Knox replied,

Mr. Herrick is quite right about running like rabbits; as anyone who has lived through a war or two has done so more than once – sometimes it is the right thing to do. But only discipline, organisation and a proper chain of command will enable troops who have run like rabbits to reform and consolidate; the anarchists had none of these things, in fact they despised them.

The People Armed.   The book *The People Armed*, a biography of Durruti published by Black Rose Press, arrived from Cam.

I have just had a real blockbuster of a paper accepted but the title was rejected. I thought the title 'Dualistic Mental Processes in Hypnosis' was quite couthful. Sorry to hear that you are not considered decadent enough. Any time you want a reference on the unmitigated squalor and depravity of your mind, let me know, I'd be delighted.

The discipline of indiscipline (II).   Durruti had about 6000 men in his Column. Each group of twenty-five had a delegate. Each four groups formed a Century. There was a Committee of Centuries made up of all delegates, a Committee of Sections made up of delegates from the Centuries and finally a Column War Committee consisting of all delegates of the Sections and the General-Delegate of the Column - Durruti.

A Military Technical Council of experts made the strategic plans and submitted these to the War Committee.

The War Committee had a bureaucracy for services such as statistics, propaganda, intelligence and so on.

There were two Commando units known as the Sons of the Night and the Black Band.

The Durruti Column refused to submit to military law imposed by the Republican and Communist forces.

Orwell said that the Column was more reliable than one might have expected. Bullying and abuse were not tolerated. The normal military punishments existed but were only used for serious offences.

Durruti wanted his army to be a model for the society it was fighting to create.

Journalists would sometimes question the men of the Durruti Column: 'You claim to have no leaders yet you obey Durruti.'

The militia men always replied, 'We follow him because he behaves well.'

She begins her Grand Tour.   He received his first letter from her. 'I am in Bangkok wishing you were here with a hip flask full of brandy and some crooked conversation . . . I will be an experienced traveller by the time we meet up in Spain . . . '

It was fine cognac they'd drunk from his flask, not just brandy.

There was a new articulate confidence in her letters.

He remembered once chiding her for what he saw as her negativity and conversational passivity. He'd shouted at her. But then he'd read Henry James' *Watch and Ward* - a novel about a thirty-year-old man who adopts a ten-year-old girl to raise as his wife. The narrator finds the adolescent girl 'defiantly torpid' but then realises that 'her listless quietude covered a great deal of observation and that growing may be a soundless process'.

The death of Durruti.   There were a number of stories about the death of Durruti - that he accidentally shot himself with his own rifle, that he was shot by an 'uncontrollable' who resented any discipline including even the discipline of indiscipline. But his chauffeur said that he was hit by a stray bullet during the battle for the University of Madrid.

Durruti was taken to the Ritz Hotel, then being used as an anarchist hospital, where he died on November 21, aged forty.

An anarchist funeral.   Before the funeral the sculptor Victoriano Macho came with other artists of the Intellectual Alliance to make a death mask of Durruti.

Hans Kaminski, a German journalist, described the funeral.

It is calculated that one inhabitant out of every four lined the streets. It was grandiose, sublime, and strange. Because no one led the crowds there was no order or organisation. Nothing worked and the chaos was indescribable . . . Durruti, covered by a red and black flag, left the house on the shoulders of the militia men from his Column. The masses raised their fists in a last salute. The anarchist song *Son of the People* was chanted. It was a moving moment. But by mistake two orchestras had been asked to come . . . one played mutedly, the other very loud, and they didn't manage to maintain the rhythm . . . the orchestras played again and again the same song; they played without paying attention to each other . . . the crowds were uncontrollable and the coffin couldn't move . . . the musicians were dispersed but kept reforming, claiming the right to play. The cars carrying the wreaths could not go forward and were forced to drive in reverse . . . it was an anarchist burial – that was its majesty.

The location of the graves.   Levine wrote,

the place to which I make my pilgrimage is the grave of Durruti which sits between the graves of Ferrer Guardia and Ascaso. How to find it? In the Great Cemetery behind the fortress is a small Protestant burial ground. Between the bulk of the Catholic Cemetery and this little annex is a spot at the edge of a hill and there three graves sit, the gravestones having been removed. But people come secretly and write on these dry concrete slabs 'CNT' and 'FAI', 'Viva anarquista' and the names. It was illegal to take photographs of the graves . . .

Two old picnickers directed Levine to the graves.

'Durruti,' said the man, 'I was on his side.'

The old woman hushed him.

Francisco, I'll bring you red carnations. In Levine's poem for Durruti's closest friend Ascaso, he says that Ascaso was a stone, Durruti a blade.

. . . the first grinding and sharpening
the other . . .
in the last photograph
taken less than an hour before
he died, he stands in a dark
suit, smoking, a rifle slung
behind his shoulder, and glances
sideways at the camera
half smiling . . .

The card, 'I have fallen in love'. A card arrived from London showing *Ulysses deriding Polyphemus* by Turner. It showed Ulysses and his men escaping in their ships from the blinded Polyphemus who, silhouetted against the sky, is throwing rocks at them (see Book IX of the *Odyssey*). They were escaping from the land of the Cyclops, 'a fierce uncivilised people who never lift a hand to plant or plough, . . . have no assemblies for the making of laws, nor any settled customs. . . '

She was now in London on her Grand Tour and the card said with irony, 'I am sorry but I can't go with you to Spain. I have fallen in love and decided to "settle down". I am, after all, twenty-one now.' She had written in as a second thought, 'Please do not communicate for now.'

Once he had bumblingly tried to describe their relationship to her, to give it shape. She had stopped him, saying, 'It is a love without definition but not without art.'

He studied the card. Was she escaping from him, a blinded Polyphemus?

Spanish Refugee Aid. Anarchists fought not only in the armies of the Spanish Republic but also in the Second World War, some in the French resistance, others as regulars in the Division Le Clerc. Some of them are still refugees unable or unwilling to go back to Spain after all these years. The old and the infirm are looked after by an organisation called Spanish Refugee Aid. Contributions can be sent to SRA Inc, 80 E 11 St, NY, NY 10003.

How did the card affect him?   He had often tried to describe to her the distinction between his attraction to her as a 'person' and his attraction to her as an 'archetype'. She had been a perfect example of 'the beautiful young girl'. And he had seen her growing as a person. She was probably right that the archetype was now left behind. She was right to have forebodings about him dying in the Hotel de la Gloria. They had talked about suicide. When he had discussed the pilgrimage with her he had thought, but not said, that he really might die there in the Hotel de la Gloria, that that might be a good point to conclude it.

Now she had diverted him from that appointment with the Hotel de la Gloria.

Compensation for angst.   He had told her once on a beach during one of her depressions that he'd found a lot of good things in life which compensated for angst. She'd said, 'Oh yeah, what are they?'

He'd told her of the surprises and serendipity of the life of inquiry, the unimaginable twistings of sexuality, about the infinite imagination, endless storytelling and its works, about the weary exhilaration of negotiation, the lateral elegance of the deal, and about the revelations of hunting and of the camp.

'But you once said *volupté* was the only solace!' she said, laughing at him.

'That too.'

What would he be able to tell her now, now that he was forty?

He'd have to say that, while all those things were still true, on some days it was only a tepid curiosity and a tired–hearted buccaneering which carried him on. But maybe they could explore the discipline of indiscipline together. And he could show her how their relationship had become two footnotes to a poem.

• THE GREAT-GRANDMOTHER • REPLICA

'And what is a gutter slut?' he asked her.

Belle considered her reply, a frown of concentration coming to her face, the face of a woman in her late twenties but carrying still the pore-less baby face of a ten-year-old and the shining eyes of a teenager. And then she said, 'A promiscuous person can sometimes be driven by a neurotic need for approval, for an affirmation through sexual contact that they are a "person" or that they are "a lovable person". They are taking a poll of all the people of the world. I don't knock that. A slut though, is a person who enjoys – well, "enjoy" may be too insipid a word – who seeks with a curiosity and vigour powered by lust – seeks to be lost, if only momentarily, in the full reaches of their generalised sexuality, if you follow me, sexuality in all its darkest, anonymous parts. This can be approached by promiscuity but that is not the only route. A slut may begin from a number of starting points, from being an unhappily promiscuous boy or girl or a person seeking defilement as a way of self-punishment. But a true slut has passed from these needs, while still being able to enjoy the theatre of these needs – say, of self-defilement – but has moved on to the larger journey to which there is no end.'

'But I asked about gutter sluts,' he said.

15

'I'm coming to that,' she said, with a tutorial tone, 'a gutter slut –
nostalgie de la boue – is the slut who prefers – or is at that point
of the journey – which involves sexual life at its lowest, the dirtiest,
the poorest, the most physically disgusting – either people or
situations or even maybe just ambience . . . '

'But why?' he broke in, 'why is this part of the journey?'

' . . . you are too impatient,' she said, 'and if you don't understand it
is because you have not yet reached this point. It is part of the journey
because it is *there*. There are sexual ambiences which belong with
social class and even with occupations. With butchers, for example.
The slut is curious. The slut must go there.'

'But didn't Gertrude Stein say that when you get there there is no
there there?'

'Believe me, pet, when you are sluttishly *there* you know you are
there.'

Once after sex Belle began to cry and he was surprised.

'Hey! I thought expeditioners didn't cry.'

'Even sluts get the blues,' she said.

Belle laughed and said, 'Good one!' when in the film *Outrageous* a
white drag queen who picks up a black in a bar says to the black, 'I'm
an equal opportunity slut.' Belle commented that sluts were into equal
opportunity before any of the political people. You could say that a
gutter slut was into affirmative action.

The drag queen in the film befriends a schizophrenic girl who
wants to have a child by a Yellow Cab driver – any Yellow Cab
driver.

'For whatever reason,' Belle said, after the film, 'schizoids make
good sluts – and I said schizoids not schizophrenics. And I'm not
valorising mental illness either. It's a fact from my experience.'

Once in bed they were playing with a Luger pistol (Navy, Second
World War). Belle liked the feel of the cold metal on her flesh, the
gun–oil smell, the lethality, the sinister aura of German pistols. It had
belonged to Belle's German father and she had given it to him. He
asked about the Nazis and what she felt when she and he played Nazi
games.

'Oh,' she said, choosing her words carefully, acknowledging the sensitivity of it, while, he thought, not wanting to leach away any of the game's spirit, 'oh Nazis are useful. They gave us a lot of good sado-masochistic imagery – they were good with costume, very good, they understood leather – but they didn't *invent* the gothic. And they were into the barbaric – not the sensual – and therefore got it all very wrong.'

'How does it fit with sluttishness?'

'It fits with sluttishness because sluttishness steals from the Nazis. Sluttishness steals fantasies and paraphernalia from anywhere. It can take items of evil and make them accessories of sensuality, turn them to things of play.'

'I am not a tart,' Belle said, playfully when he asked her about the difference between a tart and a slut, 'I'm a flan.' And added, 'I also possess *flâneur.*'

She did not bother with the question.

'A slut can never betray another slut,' Belle announced over dinner at the Hydro Majestic Hotel.

They were searching for psychic traces of his great-grandmother in the depressed, run-down, turn-of-the-century health resort district around Katoomba, 'because between two sluts all things are permitted. To revel in the recounting of one's deeds is an act of sluttishness itself. In a close relationship between two sluts it must be expected that each will want to now and then go off on an adventure. But the adventure must be brought back into the lore of the relationship.'

They were walking back along a Katoomba street past the once fashionable guest houses where his great-grandmother had operated. They saw a blonde woman checking her mail box.

'She's a slut,' Belle said, cautioning.

The woman's face was case-hardened by the Australian sun. Her long blonde hair was trained around her face to reduce the visible skin, to conceal the sun-damaged skin. But she used her hair tantalisingly like a veil so that it became an invitation to her suggested charms. The woman's eyes slyly roved them, almost molesting them, as they approached. He saw immediately what Belle meant.

'She's a beach slut,' Belle said, *sotto voce*, 'it's not only the way she uses her hair but sunbathing makes people very aware of their skins. Beach sluts move differently inside their skins. And she's aware of us – two other sluts. Like a dog she doesn't have to look closely, she senses us.'

Belle's voice had dropped to a hush and she touched his arm in warning. 'Avoid making eye contact with her or the three of us will end up rutting right here and now in the gutter.'

They kept their eyes averted and passed by.

When they were clear, Belle said, 'It would have happened in a flash if our eyes had met, we would not have known how it happened, it would have been a conflagration of souls. But I'm not up to conflagration of souls today.'

'I believe you,' he said, feeling that he had passed by an invitation of unspeakable consequence.

'You'd better believe me,' Belle said.

Belle and he stopped and peered into the run–down, vandalised lobby of a former guest house of the twenties.

Flaps hung off the mail boxes, human turds littered the floor, and the place had the odour of human urine.

A disused office with a frosted glass door with the word 'concierge' and wall lights behind picket panels of pink and green pastel glass – mostly missing – were reminders of the guest house's time of grandeur. Declined grandeur in old buildings gave him a delightful apprehension. 'It's a door to the past which I feel I can almost squeeze through. Certain buildings and their contents should be designated to be left as they were, completely untouched.'

'These old "guest houses" are of course a metaphor for this great-grandmother who has so bewitched you,' Belle said.

She looked at him then, seductively, there in the lobby of the vandalised guest house there amid the urine and excreta smells.

'Let me embody that metaphor.' She raised her skirt.

Leaning against the door they had sex, and after she wiped herself with a tissue and threw it into the lobby.

'In Egypt,' he said, as they walked back out into the street of depressed curio shops and closed-up spas, clattering with his great-grandmother's carriage and the last days of laughing tour parties, 'I was carefully keeping my rubbish inside the car – in those Hertz rubbish bags – and I kept all my empty beer bottles and Evian water bottles inside the car. One day I stopped at what appeared to be a splendid Mediterranean beach but when I went onto the beach I found it totally littered. I looked around the countryside for the first time and realised that the whole of Egypt was a rubbish tip many thousands of years old. It is a completely littered country. I then took the rubbish from my Hertz bags and my empty bottles and dumped them out in the desert with all the other rubbish. It gave me a liberating pleasure to be untidy.'

'I taught you the joy of throwing beer cans from car windows,' Belle said, 'I taught you that it was not only rule-breaking but also a simple expressive physical act of exuberant disorder. It's physical haiku which says "we pass this way but once and to hell with it".'

'But we do pass that way again, usually,' he said.

'Oh don't be wet,' Belle said. But a little later added, 'It must be done with a feeling of exuberance. Not habitually. If you feel no exuberance, don't do it.'

Belle told him that she had known he was a slut from the moment she had looked into his face.

'I knew you were too,' he said.

'That did not require masterly powers of observation,' she said, 'women sluts have many more ways of displaying it. You have to be a master-slut to pick men sluts. Since puberty – before puberty! – men have been able to look at me and tell – and I knew myself from an early age. Always look for a puffy, bruised look around the eyes or lips – it's a sort of tumescence – *embouchement* – an almost permanent tumescence of the labia which transfers itself to around the eyes and mouth. The pout. Do you know what the pout is? The pout is the face's way of mimicking the tumescent vagina. Deportment. See how I sit? That's the way a slut sits.'

'And choice of jewellery,' he said, 'there is a slut aesthetic.'

'No,' Belle said, pedantically, 'before that – I'm talking of school kids – you'll find all the signs at that age. Admittedly girl sluts are the first into jewellery. But I could go along a line of boys and girls and pick out the sluts.'

'And hence from photographs also.'

'Yes, from all those photographs of your great-grandmother and her clients at the caves, I could tell. Oh yes, I could tell.'

• • •

Belle said that people were wrong if they thought all whores were sluts. Some whores were sluts, some sluts were whores. But sluts used sexuality to extinguish self, which could only happen when you crossed the lines into the dark country where the rules were either unknown or always reversible.

'Sluttishness is a sexual insurrection of considerable degree.'

'What about Severine in *Belle de Jour*?' he asked. 'Was she a slut or just a whore or what?'

'Thrill-seeking is a sufficient justification.'

'You are capable of most sluttish things,' Belle said, 'but you can never experience the rich.'

'How so?'

'It is because you came from a wealthy background – your great-grandmother's money – you cannot get the plummeting frisson of debasing yourself before the rich. You are denied the having of sex in the shadow of fear and bewilderment. The upper-class rich can intimidate me in a way that you will never know. But I am a collector and a connoisseur of intimidation and its application to sensuality. Thus the upper-class rich serve me.'

They discussed the 'banishment of the intellect' which has to occur in sluttishness.

'One of the greatest joys of sluttishness,' said Belle with shining eyes, 'is to be intimidated and used sexually by one's intellectual inferiors, to defile one's intellect by choice of sexual company.'

A still photograph of Marlon Brando from *The Wild One* caught his eyes and he thought, 'Oh, oh – there's a slut all right. I must show this to Belle.'

In an article not in any way related to the photograph, on the same day, he came across the words, 'Brando's heavy-lidded slut in *The Wild One* lusted after furtively by Lee Marvin and explicitly quoted in the erotic fantasies of Anger's *Scorpio Rising* . . . '

He and Belle had been looking for uses of the word 'slut' applied to males.

Belle was very pleased and rewarded him.

• • •

'It is not only the making of oneself sexually available to virtually anyone from an early age, it has to become the ability to pick the appropriate partner from among strangers on any given occasion for a given sexual sortie.'

'But sexual invitation is sometimes deceitful,' he argued, 'one can rarely be sure of what lies behind the invitation. Sometimes they want you to read their poems.'

'A slut never uses a sexual invitation as a way of beginning quote a full relationship unquote or as a way of having one's poems read. A slut would use the mind to seek a fully-rounded relationship, not sexuality.'

Belle said that this did not mean that when a slut was rejected by a lover he or she would not behave badly. 'They are just as likely to burn your car or put a severed dog's head in your bed. But the motive would be deprivation not jealousy.'

Belle introduced her friend Renée as a 'trainee slut' to the visiting American poet, Mark Strand.

Belle's favourite character in history was, of course, Messalina. They were looking at Beardsley's illustration of Juvenal's *Sixth Satire* which Elwyn Lynn described as, 'Evil . . . energetically attractive or repulsive, elegant or lurching, brutally like Messalina . . .'

Belle objected, in a letter to Elwyn Lynn, about the introduction of the word 'brutally' into the description of Messalina. She said brutalisation occurred when motives other than sensual pleasure interfered with the activity.

Messalina, Belle explained, as the wife of Claudius worked in a brothel while Claudius slept, just like Severine, and was reputed not to have taken a break during her shift, always being the last to leave.

He told Belle that he'd found out that his great-grandmother sometimes took part in mock marriages with gold miners who had struck gold. They would dress in formal clothing, hold a lavish reception, a mock religious marriage service, and then the consummation in the church in front of the guests. It was a high form of whore-theatre, desecrating marriage.

'I like it, I like it,' Belle said, smiling. 'Without a doubt I am part of your ancestral theatre, I come from a line which stretches back through your great-grandmother to Messalina. 'Your seeking of your great-grandmother, your seeking of psychic traces, is a sluttish thing to do too. What I can't understand is why you can't just have a whore mother fixation, why do you have to have a whore great-grandmother?'

Among her many theories, Belle believed that we are parcel of our ancestors and that our friends and lovers are the projections of long-dead ancestors.

At the Katoomba cemetery, Belle posed at the grave of his great-grandmother.

'Is this the way you want me?' Belle asked. 'Is my sweater pulled tight enough over my nipples? Are my leotards tight into my crutch? Are my legs apart just enough to suggest unresisting submission? Are my lips pouting teasingly? Is my pelvis thrust forward enough as an invitation to enter me?'

She was not acting and her sluttish pose was no parody. He took her photograph against the gravestone which had his great-grandmother's name, the dates and the inscription, 'Not changed but glorified'.

She then came to him there in the cemetery saying, 'Let me be your great-grandmother who at seventeen whored in this old resort town and for whom you're searching.'

As he embraced her there in the cemetery he realised why he'd taken her into the heartlands on his fortieth birthday and that even if she wasn't the full story, she was maybe a replica. Whatever she was for him felt all right.

• FROM A BUSH LOG BOOK 1 •

That Christmas he went into the Budawang Ranges with his decadent friend, Belle.

They had debauched in motel rooms and restaurants along the coast while he turned forty, bed sheets drenched with champagne and with all the smells and fluids that two bodies could be made offer up in such dark love-making as, in their curious way, he and Belle were drawn into. But the conversations in the restaurants had become unproductively sadistic as they exhausted amiable conversation.

He'd gone increasingly into interior conversation with himself about 'turning forty' because she was too young to have empathy with his turning forty. And he was trying to salve the loss of his young girl-friend who was overseas and 'in love'.

He also had some home-yearnings which came on at Christmas. His family was not in town for this Christmas, but anyhow his home-yearnings had been displaced over the years away from his family in the town to the bush about fifty kilometres away from, but behind, the coastal town where he had grown up – the Sassafras bush in the Budawang Ranges.

He'd put camping gear in the car when they'd left the city and they drove as deep into the bush as the road permitted and then left the car and backpacked their way.

As they walked deeper into the bush he kept glancing at Belle to see if she was being affected by the dull warm day and the bush. He knew the creeping hysteria and dread which the Australian bush could bring about.

She saw him looking back at her and said, 'I'm coping. Stop looking back at me all the time.'

They walked for an hour or so and came to what is called Mitchell Lookout.

'This is called Mitchell Lookout,' he said, 'but as you can see it is not a lookout in the Rotary sense.'

It was a shelf of rock with a limited view of the gorge.

'Lookouts are an eighteenth–century European act of nature worship which Rotary clubs have carried on. The growth is too thick – you can't see the river down there. You'll have to take my word for it.'

'I can see that the growth is too thick.'

'Laughably, the only thing you can see clearly from Mitchell Lookout is directly across the gorge – they could have another lookout which looked across at Mitchell Lookout.'

He saw her look across at the other side and back again. She made a small movement of her mouth to show that she didn't think it was particularly 'laughable'.

'I don't go into the bush for views,' he said.

'Tell me – what do you go into the bush for?'

'I go into the bush to be swallowed whole. I don't go into the bush to look at curious natural formations – I don't marvel at God's handiwork.'

For reasons he could not explain and did not record in his log book, he decided to put the tent on the rock ledge overlooking the gorge.

'You'll find sleeping on the rock is OK,' he said, 'it is really much better than you imagine.'

'If you say so,' she said, dumping her backpack.

'I go into the bush for raw unanalysed sensory experience,' he said, 'I don't go in for naming things geologically or birds and so on.'

'You don't have to apologise for not knowing the names of the birds and the stones.'

He cut some bracken fern to lie on, more as a gesture towards the idea of what made for comfort.

'That'll do a fat amount of good,' Belle said.

'It's a gesture.'

He put up the tent, pinning each corner from inside with rocks and tying the guy ropes to rocks.

'I've even used rocks as pillows,' he said.

She sat, one leg crossed over the other, cleaning dirt from her painted fingernails with a nail file.

He instantly doubted whether she had ever used a rock for a pillow and whether sleeping on rock was in fact OK.

'There,' he said, 'the tent is up.'

She looked across at it, got up, went over and looked inside the tent but did not go in.

'How about a drink?' he said.

'Sure it's the happy hour. Any hour can be a happy hour.' She laughed at this to herself.

He went about getting the drink.

'I'll cook the Christmas dinner. That'll be my contribution.' she said.

'No,' he said, 'that's OK I'm used to cooking on camp fires.'

'Look – you may be fourth-generation Australian but you're not the only one who can cook on a camp fire, for godsake.'

'All right, all right.'

As they had their bourbons he doubted whether she could cook on campfires. He thought about what they could salvage to eat.

'I came through the Australian experience too,' she said.

'Do you know what to do if you get lost in the bush?' he asked her.

'No, I didn't mean to invite a test, but you tell me, what do I do if I get lost in the bush?'

'You stay where you are, mix a dry martini and within minutes someone will be there telling you that you're doing it wrong.'

'Ha ha. Wouldn't mind a martini now this very minute.

He had never seen her cook a meal. It was always restaurants and luxury hotels, that was their relationship.

'But it was my idea to come out here in the bush – let me cook it.'

'I'll cook it.'

'OK – if you feel happy about it.'

'I feel quite happy about it, Hemingway.'

She made a low, slow fire, just right, and rested the pannikins and camp cooking dishes on the coals. It wasn't quite the way he would have done it but he didn't say anything.

Wood coals look stable until things tilt and spill as the wood burns away.

She squatted there at the fire. She first put potatoes on the coals. She put on the rabbit pieces – which they had not themselves hunted, he hadn't brought the guns – after smearing them with mustard and muttered to herself '*lapin moutarde*', laughing to herself. She wrapped the rabbit in tin foil and wormed the pieces down into the coals with a flat stick. Then she crossed herself. She put the corn cobs on to boil, candied the carrots with sugar sachets from the motel, put on the beans. She then heated the lobster bisque, throwing in a dash of her bloody mary, again saying something to herself that he didn't catch.

Maybe a gypsy incantation.

She put the plum pudding on to be warmed and mixed a careful custard.

She squatted there at the smoking fire, stirring and moving the pots as needed, throwing on a piece of wood at the back at the right time for some quick heat, all with what he thought was primitive control. He swigged bourbon from a First World War officer's flask and passed it to her from time to time. He liked to think that the flask had belonged to one of his great-grandmother's lovers. She squatted there in silence, full of attention for what she was doing.

He swigged the bourbon and, from time to time, became a First World World officer. She had slipped into a posture which belonged to the primitive way of doing things – what? – a few thousand years ago when the race cooked on camp fires. Or more recently, back to Settlement.

He sat off on a rock and took some bearings using his Swiss compass and Department of Mapping 1:25 000 topographic maps, trying to identify some of the distant peaks.

'Shrouded God's Mountain,' he said.

'Good,' she said, not looking up.

He kept glancing at her, enjoying her postures.

He opened a bottle of 1968 Coonawarra Cabernet Shiraz.

'It's ready,' she said, muttering something.

She presented the meal with perfect timing, everything right, at the right time, no over-cooking, no cold food, no ash or grit in the food. She served it on the disposable plates they'd bought.

He complimented her.

'Don't sound so surprised,' she said.

They ate their Christmas dinner and drank the wine in the Guzzini goblets he'd bought for camping, and as they did, a white mist filled the gorge and stopped short of where they were so that they were atop of it, as if looking out the window of an aircraft above the clouds.

It came almost level with the slab where they were camped and were eating.

'Jesus, that's nice,' he said, staring down at the mist.

'I thought you didn't go in for God's handiwork.'

'Well I don't go searching for it. When he does it before my very eyes, I can be appreciative.'

She looked down at the mist while chewing the meat off a rabbit bone, as if assessing the mist, aesthetically? theologically? She ate the meal with her fingers, with their painted nails.

'It's all right,' she said, emphatically.

It was warm and there were bush flies which worried her and she kept brushing them away with her hand, cursing at them.

'Piss off you bastards,' she said.

'I've made peace with the flies,' he said. 'Sooner or later in the Australian bush you have to stop shooing the flies and let them be.'

'I'm not going to let them be,' she said, 'I'm going to give them a bad time.'

'Please yourself.'

'I will.'

'You did the meal perfectly.'

'Thank you – but you aren't the only person in Australia who can cook on a camp fire.' She then laughed, and said, 'Actually it was the first time I have cooked a meal on a camp fire.'

'It was perfect. You looked very primitive – you could have been out of the First Settlement.'

'I felt very primitive,' she said, 'if the truth be known.'

'I meant it in the best sense.'

'I assumed you did.'

They sat there with food-stained hands, smoky from the fire, food and wine on their breath. Belle exposed her legs to the misty sun.

She stared expressionlessly at him, her hand methodically waving away the flies, and she then began to remove her clothing. They had sex there on the rock slab surrounded by the mist. They played with the idea of her naked body on the rock slab, the bruising of it, the abrasion. He held her head by the hair and pinned her arms, allowing the flies to crawl over her face. She struggled but could not make enough movement to keep them off her face. She came and he came.

They drank and became drowsy watching, from a cool distance, the fire burning away.

During the night he got up because he liked to leave the tent in the dead of the night and prowl about naked. He said to himself that although he did not always feel easy in the bush, in fact, he sometimes felt discordant in it, he'd rather be out in it feeling discordant than not be there.

'What are you doing out there for godsake?' Belle called from the tent.

'Having a piss.'

He crawled back into the tent.

'I thought for a moment you were communing,' she said.

'Just checking the boundaries.'

In the morning he said, 'Well, it wasn't unsleepable on the rock.'

'No, not unsleepable,' she said, and smiled, 'not unfuckable either.'

'The rock tells our body things our mind cannot comprehend.'

'Don't give me that bullshit.'

It was still misty and the air heavy with moisture but it was not cold.

Neither of them now wanted to stay longer in the bush although they'd talked initially of staying 'for a few days'.

He thought he might have stayed on if he'd been alone.

They struck camp.

'I liked having if off on the rock,' she said, 'I seem to be bruised.'

'But you were bruised enough?' he ritualistically asked, resolving that he would not make that joke again because of its tiredness, resisting what the tiredness meant about their relationship.

'Hah, hah.'

It was a grey sky. The dampness quietened everything down just a little more than usual and the dull sky dulled everything a little more, including their mood.

They hoisted on their backpacks and began walking.

'I know all about abjection and self-esteem but for a slut like me it's all a game now.'

He gestured to indicate that he wasn't making judgements about it.

'It's no longer the whole damned basis of my personality,' she said.

'You have to be a bit like that to go into the bush anyhow. It's very easy to make it self-punishing.'

'I was thinking that.'

They walked a few metres apart. They passed a stand of grey kangaroos some way off which speculatively watched them walk by. Belle and he indicated to each other by a glance that they'd seen the kangaroos.

'More of God's handiwork,' she called.

He realised as they walked out that he had a disquiet about being there with Belle. When he looked at the Christmas they'd just had together – on paper – it was untroubled, memorable, an enriched event – the mist in the gorge, the perfect camp-fire meal, the good wine. Belle naked on the rock, his standing on the ledge in the dead of night, the melancholy bush.

The disquiet came because Belle had been moved *out of place* in his life. The Budawang bush was the place of his childhood testing, his family's bush experience, touching base, touching primitive base. He had learned his masculinity here.

She did not belong in that album.

He looked back at her up the trail, plodding through the swampy part in her Keds dripping wet from the moisture of the bushes. He saw her again at the camp fire, primitively squatting. He felt a huge fondness for her.

They'd often said that they were not the sort of person either would really choose to spend Christmas or birthdays with, they were making do with each other.

By bringing Belle with him on his fortieth birthday and on Christmas he had left an ineradicable and inappropriate memory trace across the countryside.

But she was also somehow an embodiment of his great-grandmother, they'd divined that in Katoomba at his great-grandmother's grave. But this was not his great-grandmother's territory.

He was then struck by a splintering observation – the Budawangs and the Blue Mountains of Katoomba were part of the Great Dividing Range but in his head they were different mountains, different districts. His great-grandmother and Belle belonged at Katoomba, the decayed health resort and spa. It was there that his great-grandmother had used her charms and beauty to make her living, her fortune. The Budawangs were where he'd been the boy scout and the army officer.

The parts still didn't quite come together.

He caught up with Belle and touched her fondly.

'Sorry about the mud,' he said.

'I can cope. I can take it.'

This was where he'd learned as a boy how to 'take it'.

'I'll get you a new pair of Keds.'

'They come from the States.'

'I'll get a pair sent across.'
'You probably won't.'

In a motel on the coast they showered off the mud, dried off the
dampness, turned up the air-conditioner to warm and got slowly
drunk, sprawled on the floor. Belle with a towel wrapped around her
drying hair, in a silk kimono, was like a cat back in habitat.

He spread out the map of southern New South Wales.

These are my heartlands, he showed her, the English damp green
tablelands of Bowral and Moss Vale, the old goldfields, the lakes of
Jindabyne, the new snow resort, down to Bega where my father
introduced me to the man who had a library of a thousand books of
mystery and the supernatural, to Kiama where my girlfriend from
school and I went for our miserable honeymoon after we married in
the hometown Church of England.

And Milton, where I found ten years of *Champion* magazine in an
old newsagency.

He told her how he had been a rebellious but highly proficient
scout, had played football up and down the coast, had been a soldier
on manoeuvres there, had surfed the whole coast, camped out and
hunted in all the bush.

'You're a very sentimental person,' she said, as she rubbed cream
into a scratch on her leg.

'No, I don't think I am.'

'I think you are.'

'I think not.'

'A sentimental drunk, then.'

'There is another territory.'

He circled the Katoomba and Jenolan Caves district.

'My great-grandmother's territory.'

'We've done that.'

'And there is my grandfather's territory.' He circled the town. 'He
committed suicide in the hotel there. But that was not his territory,
maybe being what he was he had no territory.'

But neither were ever mentioned in this territory, he told her,
pointing at the first heartlands circle.

Belle was leaning on his shoulder pretending an interest, for an
instant she became someone else leaning on his shoulder looking at the
map, a high-spirited late arrival at a dying party.

'Let's go,' he said, 'let's check out now and go back to the city. I think it's over.'

Two weeks later he went back to the Budawangs and camped again in the same place, alone. It was a trip to erase the mistake of having gone there with Belle.

He realised, as he sat there in the bush at Mitchell Lookout, that it was a misguided effort. Coming back to erase it had only more deeply inscribed it.

Now whenever he passed the place he would think of having gone there with the wrong person, of having taken his great-grandmother into the hard country where she didn't belong. He would laugh about Belle, squatting there cooking, about the flies on her face, and Belle saying, 'I feel quite happy about it, Hemingway.'

• FROM A BUSH LOG BOOK 2 •

He said on the telephone that he would be using a German solid-fuel stove in the bush.

'I'll put your father on,' his seventy-year-old mother said, and he pictured them passing the telephone between them, and he heard her say to his father in a very audible conspiratorial whisper, 'He says he is going to use a German solid-fuel stove.' His father came on and said the German solid-fuel stove or any-nationality-fuel stoves were banned.

What he didn't say to his father and mother was that he intended to have camp fires regardless of the fire bans. He was now forty and could damn well light a fire, legal or illegal, if he damn well wanted to. And they were disappointing him too with this fire panic. They were bush people who'd brought him up on bush codes of perseverance and on all the bush drills. Why else as a little boy had he crouched shivering and sodden at damp, smoking camp fires blowing his very soul into the fire to get it to flame. Or suffered fly-pestered pink-eye and heat headaches in the dust of summer scout camps, his ears ringing with the madness of cicadas in the hot eucalyptus air, doggedly going about his camp routines. He'd paid. And his family always lit correct fires that caught with the first match. His family knew that the bigger the fire the bigger the fool. He and his family had a pretty good relationship with fire.

On the way through to the bush he paid them a postponed Christmas visit. It was in fact his second trip to the Budawangs in two weeks. For Christmas he'd gone to the Budawangs with Belle but now felt he needed to go there alone. He wanted now to apologise to the bush for having taken Belle there. Belle had been wrong. Belle belonged in the Intercontinental. No, that wasn't really it, he wasn't sure why he wanted to go back into the bush again alone. He'd apologised to Belle for having taken her into the bush where she didn't belong.

As he stopped in the driveway of the family home they came out from the sunroom where they'd been waiting for him. His father leaned in the car window and said, 'It's a ticking bomb out there.'

His mother wanted to organise another Christmas dinner, to repeat Christmas for him.

He begged off, 'I've done a lot of moving about this year - I had my report to do - I have to go back to Canberra to present it to a standing committee - I just need to for a few days - no people. It's for the good of my soul.'

His mother understood soul.

'We expected you for Christmas,' his father said, 'I can't see what could be more important than family Christmas.'

What had been more important than family Christmas had been trying to forget his work on the nuclear fuel cycle, and turning forty. He'd tried with Belle and it had worked except for the bush part. He was going to try the bush part again, alone.

'It's a very silly move from a number of points of view,' his father went on as they moved into the house, 'the ban is total.'

He said he could smell rain about.

They didn't comment. His family didn't believe that you could 'smell' rain. He wasn't sure that he believed you could smell rain.

His mother wanted to freeze his steak he'd bought for the bush but he told her not to freeze it.

He asked her though to mend his jeans - as a way of giving her some part to play.

'You're old enough to know better,' his father said, punishing the newspaper with slaps of his hand.

His mother came back with her sewing basket. 'I'll mend it with especially strong cotton,' she said. 'My mother used this cotton.'

'Your mother used it - that same reel?'

'You don't use much of it,' she said to block his incredulity, 'so it never runs out.'

She mended his jeans by hand.

'You shouldn't go into the bush in old clothes,' she said, 'you don't want clothes falling apart in the bush.'

He'd not forgotten that dictum.

'I've put your steak in the freezer,' she said, biting the thread through with her teeth.

Later he excused himself from the room and removed the meat from the freezer.

After years of opposing frozen food his mother now preferred it. From pre-refrigeration days of her youth, his mother now obsessively feared 'things going bad' and in her old age froze everything.

Regardless of his wishes she put together a repeat of a family Christmas.

'What are you going to eat out there?' his nephew asked at the meal.

All questions from nephews and nieces were trick questions.

'Mainly tinned food,' he said, knowing this would lose him marks.

'You're not walking far then,' his nephew said with the smile of the experienced.

'No, I'm not walking far,' he said, an apology to the whole family for having included any tinned food for a camp. 'It's a lazy camp.'

They didn't know of such a thing.

'I've never carried a can of tinned food into the bush in my life,' his brother declared, 'freeze-dried is the go.'

'If he can carry it he can take it,' his sister said, quoting an infrequently used family dictum; used only to excuse foolishness, eccentricity. It was like an appeal to the High Court on some nearly forgotten constitutional ground. He smiled thankfully at her.

'You won't be able to heat them,' his father said, seizing on this as a way of stopping him. 'How do you think you're going to heat them with a fire ban on?'

'With this heat they'll be hot enough to eat straight out of the can.'

His father grunted.

'You'll need a hot meal in the evening,' his mother said, 'for strength.'

'I think, Mother, he's old enough to feed himself,' his sister said, again acting as his advocate.

'Run to the fire and out the other side,' his nephew said to his

father, talking across him, 'isn't that the way you handle bush fire?'
His nephew smirked, he now had him trapped in a bush fire.

'If it isn't burning on the other side,' his brother said, 'and if it
doesn't have a second front.'

'And that's if you get through the first wave of fire,' his nephew
said, with an estimating glance at him which indicated that he didn't
think he was the sort of person who would make it through the fire.

'Wet the sleeping bag, unzip it, and pull it over your head,' he said
to the nephew and brother. 'Isn't that how it's done?'

His brother said yes, if there was enough water around to wet a
sleeping bag and if the sleeping bag wasn't synthetic.

'Don't try to beat the fire uphill   –   you won't,' his nephew said.

'I wouldn't try,' he said to his nephew.

His nephew obviously thought he was the sort of person who would
try. His nephew tossed a nut into the air and caught it in his mouth.

'I know the fastest way to be found if you're lost in the bush.'

'What's that?' His nephew was sceptical.

'You stay where you are, mix a dry martini and within minutes
someone will turn up and tell you that you're mixing it wrong.'

The table looked at him unsatisfied, and he knew they hadn't got
the joke, they weren't a martini family and they blamed him, he could
tell, for making a joke outside the comfortable boundaries of their
shared lore. He'd blundered again. He didn't handle being a member
of a family very well.

'Why are you going?' his brother asked.

'Foolhardiness,' his father said.

He told them he was going to the upper reaches of the Clyde River
which he hadn't done yet in his walking. He wanted to look at Webb's
Crown, a remaining block of plateau around which the river had cut
itself on both sides, leaving Webb's Crown like a giant cake in the
middle of the river.

'It's nothing to look at,' his nephew said.

He couldn't very well say he was going into the bush to apologise to
the bush for having taken the wrong person to that part of his
metaphorical self. Or that he'd taken his great-grandmother replica
into the bush when he should've taken her to Las Vegas.

And when would he be able to go aimlessly into the bush, without
plan?

His family always worked the plan.

As a kid he'd just 'gone into the bush' and one thing suggested another, invitations were issued by caves, clearings, high points, creeks – they all called you to them.

'I'd like to go into the bush without a plan,' he said, to see how they'd jump, 'to go into the bush idly.' The word 'idly' was strange to the dining room.

'Plan the work: work the plan,' his father said.

'If you didn't have a plan how would you know where to go next?' asked his nephew.

An existential question.

'It's the journey not the destination,' his ever–protective sister said.

He thought it was both. But he didn't want to have her offside too. 'I hated all that up–at–dawn, fifty–kilometre–day regimented walking we all went in for as kids,' she added.

As he was putting his things into the car the next day his mother gave him a two–litre plastic container of water and told him to put it in his pack.

It wouldn't fit in his pack but he told her he was going, anyhow, to the river.

He tried to ask casually, 'Which side of the family were bushwalkers – was grandmother a bushwalker?' he asked.

'Oh no,' she said, 'she was a city lass.'

'Great–grandmother?' He knew the standard answer.

'She's a bit of an unknown quantity,' she said, 'she lived in Katoomba and that's about all we know. She worked at the Caves.'

He wondered again if that was all she knew. He never got further than that answer.

His father wouldn't come out to say goodbye. His going into the bush in direct refusal of an order.

His mother said she would pray for rain.

'Well don't flood the river on me,' he said.

He drove as far as he could into the bush and then, hoisting his pack, left the car – going through the Act of Severance, the break with habitation and people, the solitary swimming out into the wilderness.

For him it always required a mustering of will and it always brought about a tight alertness. He'd taken 15 mg of Serepax on the drive up to the bush to counteract his family's sapping and to calm him for the bush.

He's taking drugs, his nephew said.

But the tightness continued. Again, as always, the small cold warning spot of fear switched on as the connections with safety receded.

As he walked deeper into the bush his mind monitored his system, running over his body like a hand, a detector listening for fault.

The bush flies were thick but he'd seen them thicker and anyhow he'd make a détente with the flies. He said peace to the flies, peace.

He talks to the flies.

He came to the slab of rock and he laughed to himself about making love to Belle, holding her so the flies crawled over her face. There were three kinds of flies this time, he noticed, which he wasn't allowing to bother him.

Something about fucking a girl on the rock and flies.

As he stood on the slab and recalled the perfect Christmas dinner she'd cooked, he realised that his efforts this time to somehow 'erase' the mistake of bringing Belle into the bush was not going to work. He had inscribed it deeper by doing it. And it didn't worry him now anyhow. She was maybe a re-enactment of his great-grandmother and that was that. Whatever that meant.

He's not going on about the great-grandmother again?

He decided to go down into the gorge by way of a descending creek, barely running, which led him to a rainforest on the slope of the gorge. Vines, moss, a dense overhead canopy of branches and vines, silence. He liked the dank chambers of rainforest – they were like a nightclub in the daytime, broken sunlight, a smell of trapped staleness. He sat for a while in the dankness. The flies would not come there.

Maybe this is where Belle and he should have come for Christmas. Or maybe this was where he should lie down and never rise, there in the decay.

He wants to lie down in all the crap.

But he went on, down the remaining stretch of creek, blocked here and there with boulders, and then dropping steeply to the river. Reaching the river was a minor exultation. It was no great river at this point but it ran with enthusiasm and had a thin waterfall. He stood under the fall naked – waterfalls, however thin, always suggest that you watch them or stand under them.

He's standing there under the waterfall testing a notepad of waterproof paper.

After two hours or so of more walking he began to lose alertness and decided to make camp.

He wasn't a follower of the Fung Shui approach to camp sites, the search for the most propitious site. He accepted 'good' camp sites when they came around the corner – the running creek, the camping cave, the grassy knoll. But most of all he liked making camp in unpromising situations. He liked to shape an unpromising site into shelter. Sometimes he was reluctant to leave those camps he'd won from rough conditions. He supposed this was 'very Western'. He used to say in restaurants back in Sydney and Vienna that he went into the bush to have a dialogue with Western Man but instead he invariably became a Man from a Western.

He took off his pack and declared 'this is it'. As the gypsies would say, anyone who now approaches this place would have to ask permission to sit by 'his' fire and should not walk between him and his fire, and should approach with sufficient noise so as not to be mistaken for a stalking enemy. But in all the years he had walked in the Australian bush he had never come across another person.

Something about gypsies, he's talking about gypsies.

There had been times when he'd fancied he heard someone 'out there' and sometimes he kept his loaded Luger pistol at hand to keep away the phantoms. There were also the times when he would have quite liked someone to come out of the bush to join him and drink bourbon at the camp fire. He heard voices at times, but knew them for what they were.

He packs iron. He packs iron!?

He built his fire in the almost dry river bed where a narrow stream of water still ran in a wide bed of sand. But when he came to light the fire he couldn't find the disposable lighter which he used in the bush. He remembered checking the equipment against the thirty-one-item equipment list before he started. He was, he thought, good at checking and constructing lists. Last year he'd bought a replica of a 1930 brass smokestone lighter from the United States for the look of it – from an Early Winters catalogue. But the fuel dried out of the smokestone lighter in the summer heat. He'd gone back to the cheap disposable lighters. But it was missing.

He went through the equipment. No lighter. From the moment you left the car behind you things began to go against you in the bush – something always got broken, something spilled, something was lost, something forgotten. Well, rarely forgotten with his drill. Everything began to degenerate – batteries, food. From the moment you left civilisation you had only so long to live.

He forgot his lighter.

His incompetence about the lighter appalled him. Fire was crucial.

He went to the emergency kit where he had a box of waterproof matches. They were there. Go on, deduct points, he said to his nephew, take off ten points.

Fifty.

He lit the camp fire.

He grilled his steak on a green forked stick, baked two potatoes in the coals. He wondered if his mother had taken the lighter from his pack. Impossible.

He for-got his ligh-ter.

He for-got his ligh-ter.

He ate two marshmallow biscuits.

After dinner he killed the fire and went up beside the tent on the grass. It was a cool evening and he thought he could detect rain in the air, a fall in barometric pressure maybe.

He settled down with a flask of Jack Daniels bourbon, sipping it from his Guzzini goblet which he carried for sipping Jack Daniels in the bush.

He wished himself a good fortieth year.

He ate smokehouse almonds. He felt the bush to be benign for the first time on this trip. He had shed the pangs of isolation. After the second bourbon an emphatic peace fell about him. He finished the evening writing languid notes – a conversation with himself, it sure as hell beat a lot of conversations he'd had that last year.

He's sloshed.

In his tent, in his sleeping bag, his torch hanging from the ceiling, he read a few pages of *Buddenbrooks*. Having run away from his own bourgeois mercantile family he immersed himself in the fortunes of Mann's German bourgeois family of the nineteenth century.

Herr Ralf von Maiboom, owner of the Pöppenrade estate, had committed suicide by shooting himself with a revolver, in the study of the manor-house. Pecuniary difficulties seem to have been the cause of the act.

'With a revolver?' Thomas Buddenbrook asked, and then, after another pause, he said in a low voice, slowly, mockingly, 'That is the nobility for you.

He says we're bourgeois.

During the night he was woken by rain and said to himself, 'Well done, Mother.' and drifted back to sleep with the pleasure of being in a wild environment but secured against it, he liked weathering out storms in a tent.

In the morning it was drizzling but he took out the German solid-fuel stove and set it up in a small pocket cave, the size of a fireplace, for the making of the morning coffee to begin a wet day in the bush.

Make a fuzz-stick. No need for the emergency stove just because of a little drizzle.

Well, he didn't feel like fooling around with damp wood.

Strip dead wood from standing trees.

He *knew* how to make a fire in the wet. He just wasn't going to crouch and blow his soul into a damp fire.

Having set up the stove he couldn't find the matches.

He went into the tent and made a cramped search through his things again, taking everything out of the backpack, and emptying the food bag.

My God, now he's lost the matches.

Dismayed, disbelieving, he sat in the tent surrounded by his thirty-one items of gear and tried to think what could have happened to the matches.

Twenty-nine items of gear.

Yes, twenty-nine items of gear, yes.

He searched the route from the tent to the dinner fire, to the side of the river course where he'd washed, to the place where he'd sat sipping his bourbon. He went to where he'd had a piss.

He considered the possibility that an animal, a possum maybe, had taken them; but he would then have expected to find remains of chewed matches. Frankly, he'd never had a possum take anything, at any camp. Once a dingo pup had taken some food from a pot. What would an animal want with waterproof matches?

He thinks a possum took them.

He crawled back into the tent, the drizzle barely making a sound on the tent, and reported to his captain-self that he'd lost the matches   – had failed to pack the lighter and then had lost the emergency matches.

He really has lost the matches.

He could perhaps do something fancy like using a magnifying glass from his monocular.

If there was sun.

Yes, if there was sun.

He hadn't mastered the bow and friction drill method. And he really didn't understand what tinder was.

Doesn't know what tinder is.

In the tent he ate all the marshmallow biscuits, dulled still with disbelief about the matches.

He eats marshmallow biscuits for breakfast. What?! He takes marshmallow biscuits into the bush!?

For godsake he was forty and he could damn well eat what he wanted for breakfast.

But they didn't make him feel good.

As he brooded, it came to him as a dim signal from a long way off that there was a conspiracy going on.

The parent within was hiding the means of making fire from the wilful child. But it was such a pedantic case of the psychopathology of everyday life. It offended him and its realisation brought him no relief.

He's saying it all has to do with Freud.

He forced himself to get out of the tent. He put on his poncho again and stood in the drizzle, dispirited. He decided to take a walk downstream for a while, maybe to Webb's Crown. But after fifteen minutes of hard going, the drizzle, the lost matches and the marshmallow breakfast broke his resolve and he gave up and began to make his way back to the camp.

'I am a Marshmallow Bushman,' he said. 'We are the Marshmallow Men. We are the stuffed men.'

He began to break camp.

Eyre, Stuart, Sturt. The explorers would not have been defeated by their mothers' magical interference.

Did his great-grandmother have a part in this? Belle, part-reincarnation of his great-grandmother. Wrong person to have brought into the bush. Painted fingernails. Painted toenails. Luxury life whore. There to apologise.

Something about the great-grandmother again.

He would go back to the city and hole up at the Intercontinental.

Ring Belle.

As he pulled down the tent he found the matches. They were under the eaves of the tent just where the fly of the tent came near to the ground. Somehow they'd fallen from his pocket the night before and bounced under the eave. They hadn't 'fallen', they'd been put there by the invisible hand of his mother.

The whole trip had been spooked. Too many relatives, living and dead, were meddling with his mind. The bush of the district was too strong a psychic field this Christmas.

He's thrown it in.

In the drizzle, he zigzagged his way up the steep, wooded slope of the gorge, hauling himself up the successive rock ledges which characterised that country.

He reached the plateau and the drizzle stopped and was replaced by a fog which came swirling in over the range. Visibility dropped to about two metres and he walked by compass.

'Stop it, Mother. You've prayed too hard. We've got fog.'

His compass brought him to the car and he congratulated himself on his navigation.

Not bad, not bad for someone who forgets the lighter and loses the matches.

He dumped his pack in the luggage compartment of the car and found the lighter lying there. He got out of his wet clothes into the dry city clothes. He combed his hair in the rear-vision mirror. He switched on the radio to music and swigged from the flask of bourbon, surrounded by white fog.

He was safe from his mother's fog and rain for the time, and from his great-grandmother's disdain for the bush, if that was what he was copping, and from the mockery of his nephew. For the time. In the car. In the fog.

• THE GRANDFATHER'S •
CURSE

His father took him to the sunroom after his mother had gone to church and from the back of a book where he'd concealed it pulled a photocopied old newspaper page.

'Now, in your forties, there is something you should know.'

His father put down his glasses as if beginning a speech.

He silently agreed, there were many things he felt he should know in his forties.

'You are approaching the age,' his father said, looking down at part of the newspaper, 'when your grandfather died.'

He reached for the photocopy.

His father did not hand it to him.

His father's face shaped into yet higher seriousness.

'Your grandfather killed himself,' His father, the retired magistrate, now looked as if he were swearing an oath. 'This is to remain a secret between us. The rest of the family know nothing. But you are nearing the age when your grandfather committed suicide and you should know.'

He reached for the photocopy, but again his father withheld it.

'I don't want the family to know,' his father enjoined.

43

He again reached for the photocopy and this time his father released it. He nodded to his father's words but his attention had gone to 1909, to the newspaper page from the country town weekly.

At first he could not see the item about his grandfather. The surrounding news competed for his attention. Airship Solution. Mr Glazebrook of Clive and eight others watched what is thought to have been an aerolite for fifteen minutes until it disappeared at Cape Kidnapper. They described it as a bright light with the brilliance of a star which kept going in the same direction but rose and fell like a bird in flight. There is a suggestion that it could have been an airship of unknown origin or an atmospheric phenomenon. Some said the sound of a machine was heard coming from the aerolite.

But then, The Tragedy in Police Gaol.

He read how his grandfather had appeared before the court in the country town charged with helpless drunkenness, and had been remanded for medical treatment. He had been drinking heavily in recent weeks.

His father didn't know why. 'The incident was never discussed at all in the time I was growing up.'

His grandfather was found dead in a padded cell of the gaol.

The report said, 'He had torn his shirt into strips and strangled himself as he lay on the bed.'

How could a person possibly do that? Was it humanly possible to strangle yourself that way?

The court was told he had been drinking heavily.

He got out of his bed at home shortly after 2 o'clock and went to the Masonic Hotel. He smashed the glass in the front door of the hotel and putting his hand in the aperture unlocked the door. He then proceeded upstairs but in so doing awoke the inmates of the hotel. The proprietor immediately rang for the police. Constable Wilson after a tough struggle, with the aid of the proprietor and two of the boarders, succeeded in getting the handcuffs on him.

The defendant showed positive signs that he was temporarily deranged as he refused to walk down stairs in the usual way, but insisted on backing down and then walking backwards into the cab. On arrival at the police station he again insisted on walking backwards and in this manner reached the lock-up. The defendant told the gaoler that he was going back in his life.

The newspaper story ended and then came a two-line advertisement for Wood's Peppermint Cure.

'I was four at the time,' his father repeated, as if absolving himself from responsibility. 'I never have informed anyone. I have never known what to do with the information.'

His father in his seventies was still trying to hide and share at the same time his unwanted secret. Why the Masonic Hotel when his father was an eminent Freemason? Why should his father be visited by malevolent coincidences at his age?

'I was researching the family,' his father said, bewildered. His father held out his hand for the photocopy of the clipping, wanting to take it back, but he did not give it to him.

And he himself was visited by the same sly coincidence, there and then in the sunroom, that he had first been dead drunk in a Masonic Hotel, another Masonic Hotel, when he was a youth.

This recollection passed across his attention and blocked out the newspaper he held in his hand for a second, and then the newspaper claimed back his attention.

Russia's new navy, death by misadventure, alleged bigamy, deplorable fatalities, sudden death, trotting club notes. The average age then for males was forty-seven. Two suicides on the pages of the small-town newspaper. Tough times.

Walking backwards, walking backwards from what? Walking back from the event. Trying to turn back time, walking backwards away from his life in that country town. How far back did his grandfather want to go? Back to London? Back before he was married?

His father said that his grandfather married late – at thirty-nine. Was this a warning to him now not to marry? Was it a curse?

What was upstairs at the Masonic Hotel that his grandfather wanted? The drink would have been downstairs. Was he looking for a friend? A male? A female? Why didn't the friend take care of him?

Maybe a room, maybe he wanted to sleep in the hotel, not go home, not be at home.

I've hunted tigers in Bengal,
And lions at Zambesi falls,
The elephant and the hippo too
The rhino and the kangaroo
But, though I am a hunter bold
I must confess I funk a cold
So when hunting I make sure
Against such risks by Wood' Peppermint Cure.

'Shouldn't it read, "by taking Wood's Peppermint Cure"?' he asked his father. 'Here,' he showed him the verse and the last line, realising that it was a nervous deflection away from the unwanted family fact. His father did not follow what he was saying, obviously unable to bring his mind away from the bewilderment of the revelation.

' "So when hunting I make sure. Against such risks by *taking* Wood's Peppermint Cure.",' he said to his father, a little more loudly.

'Oh yes, yes, yes.'

How did they rhyme cure and sure? Maybe pronunciation had changed.

Infanticide, bigamy, suicide, drunken drowning and a UFO all on one page.

And the gods striking out – 'In Johnsville lightning snaked off the double chimney of a house occupied by Mr and Mrs W. Skinner. The flash brilliantly lighted their bedroom and was followed by a deafening detonation – a 400-day clock stopped at the exact minute of the strike.'

How could he have suicided if he were that drunk?

Was his father cursing him?

Describing the laying down of the keels of four of the Russian Dreadnoughts, the *Times* correspondent in St Petersburg said, 'Great difficulties were experienced in selecting the designs. Last year the choice seemed to lie between Hamburg and Italian designs, but the superiority of those offered by the British became apparent.'

Once in the bar at UN City in Vienna, Ulyanov had asked him what 'dreadnought' meant after they'd seen it on an old English soft-drink case among garbage in the street.

Dread means fear, nought means no. No fear. Dreads nothing. Do not fear this – no – the opposite, it means fear me because I am without fear.

It was used for a British class of warship with guns of one large calibre.

And about the UFO story. He and a friend had once seen a UFO and not reported it. Back when they'd been just out of school.

They felt intellectually guilty about having *seen* it and he now felt intellectually guilty about not having spoken out about it.

They had not said anything at the time because they were unwilling to identify themselves with the sort of people they thought saw UFOs – cranks, nuts. He and Rich were Rationalists. So they had agreed they wouldn't say anything about it. 'What good would it do?' they'd asked themselves, trying to excuse their denial of the evidence of their eyes.

They had been walking down the path from a house at night when a large circular spacecraft-shaped image or thing passed over their heads at about 100 metres. It had disappeared in an instant. He and Rich turned to each other and said, 'Did you see that?' He remembered having a dry mouth.

Yes, they'd both seen it. It was a UFO. There was no report next day in the newspapers of any sightings or an explanation of what they'd seen.

When he was at school in the fifties a school teacher had tried to convince the children that UFOs were optical illusions which they could produce by staring at the back of their eyelids or by some such optical manipulation. He had tried to believe the teacher. But the trick with the eyes had been unconvincing.

He had his grandfather's temperament. But he had his great-grandmother's temperament too. Both wrestled for his soul. What was he doing believing that sort of thing? Belle talked like that.

Last year he had been backpacking in the Australian bush with an American physicist who deodorised too much and who had been given his name by an American associate, Madden, who hung about the IAEA in some capacity. During one of their rest stops he'd told her the story of the suicide.

'Is it a curse?' he'd asked her, not at all interested in her opinion.

'But I know that hotel!' she said, excitedly, 'I've been to that town when I did my Australian tourist-type trip two years ago. I stayed at that hotel.'

She belonged to that club of wandering people who moved about the world doing international civil service business in semi-loneliness, seeking the company of acquaintances, talking to strangers in bars, having slim professional connections forced by lonely circumstance to double as 'social life'. He belonged to that club. Following up whatever tenuous introductions you had in a strange city.

He said he sometimes calculated the curse differently – sometimes simply by age – that when he reached that age, forty-seven, he would be impelled to suicide, sometimes he calculated it as being the years his grandfather had been married – the married years – which was not, as he was at present unmarried, a threat to him – or sometimes he calculated it as the years he'd been away from his home town. Or it could be calculated as being operative on the fourth year of the first child, if he married and had children.

'I don't know about curses,' the American physicist said, as they hoisted up their packs and moved off.

The coincidence which grinned malevolently from the newspaper was that after he and Rich had seen the UFO he'd become falling down drunk, 'dead drunk' in another Hotel Masonic in Petersham, Australia.

He remembered being there with his friends – all around seventeen – and he remembered their remarking to one another after the second or third glass that the beer wasn't 'having any effect at all'. They were stronger than the power of alcohol.

They had for that moment, and that moment only in their lives, believed that their will was all–powerful, could overcome alcohol.

He remembered then being in a lavatory, asleep, being woken, staggering, barely standing, with his staggering friends trying to keep him on his feet.

All staggering, they'd taken him back to where he boarded and propped him up against the door and rung the bell, and stumbled off. He'd vomited over himself.

That night he'd pissed the bed – mortification upon mortification.

In the morning he'd had to face the landlady with death in his heart and his head racked with pain, and with a defeated will.

'I've wet the bed,' he said, again a child at seventeen in a voice without any strength of self.

He had faced the landlady and then taken the soiled sheets to the washing machine.

He had been unable to tell Robyn about it ever.

He'd met the curse already – on that day.

• DRINK •

Because of loss of energy – reaching for a book was an effort –
sweating, horrendous nausea, inflammation of the oesophagus, pale
shit, he went to have tests done by a GP in the city he was visiting.

The GP was grave. 'You have cirrhosis,' she said. She was appalled
at how much he drank.

'You must never drink again,' she said, studying the liver function
tests.

He'd told her that at the end of the day he had about four or five
drinks before dinner – beers, martinis, bloody marys, or bourbons
– followed by a half to full bottle of wine with dinner, followed
maybe by a glass of beer to 'refresh the palate', followed by probably
two ports or liqueurs or cognacs with coffee and then some after-
dinner drinking, say a few beers or bourbons – about twelve to
fifteen drinks of alcohol a day, each drink containing about half an
ounce of alcohol. He drank about six days a week and within a month
there would be a number of heavy drinking 'sessions' lasting over
eight hours when, apart from dinner or lunch drinks, there would be
another eight or so, bringing a session to about twenty drinks.

Not only did he find it hard to be honest about the amount he drank, sensing that it was a little gross, he also had never in his life *counted it up.*

He told his friend and drinking companion Richard that he had cirrhosis and would never drink again but Richard vehemently disputed this (after all, if one of them had cirrhosis, then all of them might!). Richard insisted that he have further tests done by a 'friendly doctor' who would give him a clean bill of health.

'But Richard,' he said, 'I *am* sick.'

The friendly doctor, himself a drinker, did liver function tests and interpreted them as 'the result of a heavy binge' and said that he'd be OK after a week off the booze.

His own GP said that if he were worried he'd refer him to a specialist.

'Yes, I'm worried,' he said.

When he told the liver disease specialist how much he drank, the specialist said, 'Hell, I drink that much.'

The specialist diagnosed viral hepatitis – a mild case – and recommended abstaining from alcohol for six months to allow any damage to the liver to repair itself.

He decided to follow this course. It was his first extended abstinence from alcohol in twenty-five years – since he'd left school.

In the first week he worried that he did not have 'friends', only drinking companions, and that he would now be unacceptable company, that he would be socially deserted.

Drinking was a ritualised bonding, mutual intoxication was an act of helpless solidarity in the face of the human condition. How was he going to face the human condition without drink?

When he was younger he had sometimes wanted to 'drink himself to death'. In literature it had seemed a romantic and pleasant way to go, imagined as a slipping into intoxication and then into death, but he realised that he had wilfully misunderstood the expression 'drinking yourself to death' and that it would be both painful and miserable.

Alcohol was like a camp fire they huddled around.

He tried the non-alcoholic drinks, noting for the first time that supermarkets carried something called non–alcoholic 'wine'. He finally settled on drinking a mix of non–alcoholic cider and soda water about fifty-fifty and became fond of it. He also drank virgin marys (bloody marys without alcohol).

Drinking companions were a special sort of friend – 'he's good to drink with' – who would go willingly with you into the zones of intoxication and anything that might follow from that.

How static he now found his personality. The weather of his days seemed mild. Alcohol, he thought, introduced an exaggerated mental turbulence and strong winds into the personality.

He observed that now sober he was more absent-minded; he'd expected the opposite. But he did find that he no longer needed to keep notes of information given to him the night before.

After a month he had his first yearning for a drink – he yearned for a cold, flavoursome American beer – a Coors in a heavy glass beer mug – with salted popcorn in a dim American country and western bar with a stool-girl to chat with.

A form of intimacy, a description of a relationship, 'We did a lot of drinking together.'

He realised that alcohol was a relatively benign drug and that after twenty-five years of consistent drinking he suffered no distressing withdrawal symptoms.

He'd always known that uneasiness with people was behind some of his drinking. This was confirmed after his first public lunch with strangers when he developed neck tension.

He dreamed that he'd forgotten he should not drink and had accepted a drink and wiped out the progress of repair that his liver had achieved.

He observed a dinner party, his first sober dinner party for years. He noticed the conversational risks that drinking encouraged, the making of puns, the wise-cracking, quipping, the saying of things which might fail. Other drinkers gave a generous reception to everything –

at least in the early part of the dinner. Drinking permitted free association, emboldened a quickfire tempo, which he found beyond his non-drinking mind. He found his mind too self-critical, full of stray material, cluttered with marginal connections, too qualified by caution. Later intoxication, he observed, was not so generous. It could become querulous, dogmatic, obsessive, and attention to what others were saying became erratic.

He decided that as a non-drinker he should leave drinkers at midnight.

He had his second craving. He craved spaghetti bolognese, plenty of cheese, plenty of black pepper, with a bottle of Valpolicella. The craving came to him while reading *Her Privates We* - First World War soldiers eating spaghetti and drinking wine behind the lines. It was not a ravenous craving.

He realised that he'd sometimes had a drink to make himself 'feel like drinking'.

When he told Louise at a restaurant dinner that he was not drinking, Louise said, 'What a bore.' and at first found it disconcerting. Maybe she felt she was being denied the security of complicity.

He was reminded of the play *The Iceman Cometh* where Hickey returns to his former drinking buddies after having found 'peace of mind' and given up drinking.

Hickey tells his former drinking mates in the saloon that he isn't against drinking though.

Just because I'm through with the stuff don't mean I'm going Prohibition. Hell, I'm not that ungrateful! It's given me too many good times . . . If anyone wanted to get drunk, if that's the only way they can be happy and feel at peace with themselves, why the hell shouldn't they? . . . I know all about that game from soup to nuts. I'm the guy that wrote the book . . .

But they find that having a sober Hickey about affects their drinking. One of them, Rocky, says, 'But it don't do no good. I can't get drunk right.'

And then Harry Hope who owns the bar, says, 'When are you going to do something about this booze, Hickey? Bejees, we all know you did something to take the life out of it! It's like drinking dishwater! We can't pass out! . . .there's no life or kick in it. . .'

• • •

In the mornings he tended still to have a slight thickness of the mind, a pain from awakening back to life which he had always attributed to slight hangover.

But whatever slight pain there was in the morning it was not as horrendous as hangover and every morning he had a dream again that he had accidentally drunk alcohol and would have to start his six months over again.

In his period of sobriety he was for the first time able to examine the nature of his drinking. He saw it as maybe, six drinking *sets* or separate waves of intoxication.

The first set of drinks, say the first three or so, achieved a perceptible change of mental weather – a change to a conscious mellowness, reasonably anxiety-free, although it had to be noted that the first drinks also usually punctuated the day and the end-of-work stress. The drinks celebrated a productive day or took the sting out of 'one hell of a day'.

The second set of drinks (say, the drinks with dinner) gave a free play to the mind, and stimulated some rush of ideas and words, a pleasing (or self-pleasing at least) rush of verbalisation.

The third set of drinks (equivalent to, say, the first of the after-dinner drinks) was simply a fuelling or maintaining of the first two waves of intoxication, the heightened animation and mellowness.

The fourth set of drinks – if embarked upon – represented for him the beginning of a pursuit of deeper relaxation or intoxication, some unspecified state of pleasure (through chance encounter, confessional conversation, uncontrolled hilarity, revelry or whatever). In recent years of drinking he'd found alcohol unreliable in achieving this effect.

The fifth set of drinks was pursuit of loss of self, a seeking of a high level of intoxication without real expectation and with no concern for the aftermath. Again, he'd found alcohol increasingly unreliable as a means of reaching this stage.

There was perhaps a sixth wave of intoxication – drinking to oblivion, passing out – which was something he had not done since his teens or early twenties.

He'd found that waves four and five could fail to occur and, instead, become sodden intoxication leading to irritability. When drinking he was now able to perceive that the potential of reaching these states was lost and that there would be no pay-off from further drinking. But with good drinking companions it was always tempting to try for the fourth and fifth state.

After three months of non-drinking he found that he still had the feeling after dinner parties that he had been 'intoxicated'. He could now observe the adrenalin effect as distinct from alcoholic stimulation. He now saw that his non-drinking personality too was *not* particularly different from his drinking personality. He still said dumb things, and, if relaxed, could still be reasonably spontaneous, outrageous, playful. His earlier observations of himself soon after he'd stopped drinking had been of a tense and self-conscious, fearful, non-drinker.

He listed the drinking experiences which he missed:
• for some reason he missed again the drinking of cold cans of beer with a friend in a car at a drive-in cinema, eating hot dogs with mustard and sauce (something he hadn't done for years).
• drinking Jack Daniel's 'old No. 7 Tennessee sour mash whiskey' and eating salted nuts on an international flight at 10 000 metres looking down on the world's terrain – say, the delta of the Ganges or the Russian steppes – or looking at the sun setting across a cloud bank, disoriented in time, ideally listening to Indian classical music in the headphones.
• champagne at intervals at the Sydney Opera House looking out onto the harbour.
• Jack Daniel's bourbon alone in a motel room in a strange city after a long journey, watching foreign television.
• a very cold Heineken beer and a Mexican meal arranged in a garden courtyard in the sun.
• Jack Daniel's beside the campfire in the bush, after a day of heavy going, on a cold night, with macadamia nuts.
• cans of West End beer off the ice while driving across the outback in a Volvo wagon on a hunting trip.
• a good cognac or a pernod and ice alone in his reading chair, with a book, in a dim room, reading for the night, with an occasional telephone call to or from a close friend.
• a correctly made, not too dry, but very very cold martini in a dim piano bar, with the pianist playing the blues.

Another dream that he had been drinking and had set back his recovery.

He'd lost the habitual urge for a drink at about six or seven at night.

He found himself searching interviews and biographies for references to drinking, how much successful people had drunk, drink and its effect on work.

He remembered how he'd felt when he'd been drinking that if he did not drink for a day or so he'd earned the right to a heavy drinking session. What would six months off the drink earn him?

The drinking 'session'.   He realised that really much of his drinking in the past had been in the form of the 'session', if not the 'spree'. Spree drinking was taking the drink wherever it might lead you in the night, unrestrained drinking as a launching pad into unrestrained behaviour. But a 'drinking session' was simply open-ended extended drinking.

He could remember the time when he'd felt that there was no point to 'a couple of drinks', that the drinking session was the only meaningful use of alcohol, 'serious drinking'.

But measured drinking, a consciously shaped intoxication, had its own hedonism, its own enchantments, especially when integrated with, say, sex.

This old lesson was nicely articulated by the eighteenth-century lawyer and bon vivant William Hickey (another Hickey) that alcohol was generally best when it was subservient to other activities and not the activity itself. Hickey said, 'I certainly have at different periods drunk very freely, sometimes to excess, but it never arose from the sheer love of wine; society – cheerful companions, and lively seducing women – always delighted and frequently proved my bane; but intoxication for itself I detested, and invariably suffered grievously from.'

But it was a damned hard lesson to remember at midnight, and it was a lesson which for him wouldn't stay learned – even after two hundred years.

He again dreamed he'd forgotten that beer was as dangerous to his recovery as any other alcohol and that he'd drunk it, setting himself back again.

He had his first sensation of agoraphobia. At an airport he'd found the concourse full of faces from plays, from films, from his past, from his own scripts and stories – the smell of the food at the tables, the rattle of dishes, machinery noises, all recalled in an overwhelming jumble other people and other places and other airports, other journeys.

A jamming of his mind with recollection. They'd all crushed in on him and he felt badly like a drink, like drinking heavily, but he resisted.

He recalled the search, in the later stages of intoxication, for the accelerating drink, the hit which would bring deep relaxation or wild loss of self. He would change drinks or order a stronger drink in the pursuit of the last grand wave of intoxication. It didn't always come.

Strangely, he sensed that his co-ordination had grown worse during the months of not drinking. He seemed to bump into things, stumbled more. He feared he had multiple sclerosis.

Maybe he'd done this when drunk too and just not noticed it.

He felt the gratification of a sense of health – loss of weight – a consciousness of fitness of being able to run further, cut more wood, walk further when backpacking. But it was by no means a dramatic increase in fitness, he had always been reasonably fit. He'd always wanted to be a 'healthy drunk'.

It was a bit like being an adolescent again.

Now when he did irrational things or said dumb things he would say to himself, 'But Jesus, I was sober!'

He feared every now and then that the non-alcoholic cider he was drinking was actually alcoholic and would re-check the label on the bottle.

He was now clearly aware of the chemicals which operated naturally in his body – he guessed they were things like adrenalin and hormonal activity – which caused excitation, agitation, senses of well-being. He could also clearly feel the effects of caffeine, msg, sugar.

He observed that sometimes sexual attraction for that which was beyond possibility – say, seeing a sexually desirable woman in the street – or lost love – could transform itself almost immediately into a desire for alcohol. He had not observed the sexual desire-alcohol link so clearly before.

The martini mystique   Louise, his first adultery, had introduced him to the martini. He missed the cold chilling seep of intoxication which came from a strong, correctly made martini, with the taste of gin distinguishable from the taste of vermouth but with the exquisite blending of both tastes in the mouth to make the martini taste, blending then again with the olive. He liked to be able to detect the vermouth in the martini, which went against the fashion for the very dry, almost 100 per cent gin martini. He also enjoyed the 'third' martini – the watery cold one left in the jug, the leftovers, which was mostly iced water with a martini flavour.

He wondered how his young wife Robyn had known about the origin of the martini. Had she had a lover back then too, who drank martinis?

The six months ended and he passed his liver function tests. His first cautious drink was a beer – a can of Carlton draught. He feared the nausea which was his last remembered reaction to alcohol. The Carlton did not taste as he wanted it to taste and he had no inclination to drink more that night but the taste did recall his first beer, drunk from a bottle at the back of a dance hall when he was a seventeen-year-old school captain – twenty-five years before.

Of all the drinking experiences he'd yearned for during his non-drinking period only the cans of beer with hot dogs in the drive-in cinema failed to live up to his expectation.

During his forced abstinence he discovered that alcohol was not needed for him to enjoy uninhibited and spontaneous sex. He found he was marginally more active in what he described as affectionate, low-key sex. But upon returning to drinking he enjoyed again the extended sexual experiences with slow drinking – any drink – over a few hours, especially with Belle.

• WHITE KNIGHT •

He explained to Sandra, a new-wave television producer, that having watched so many *Kojaks*, *Callans* and *Rockford Files* and given his experience with international nuclear intrigue, he was now 'ready to try to write a White Knight formula series for television'.

Yes, it was an old-wave idea, but this would be nuclear White Knight – a Knight who polices the new energy. And a career change.

'My whole life has been a preparation for this,' he said. 'I was not slumped there in front of your television set for those years when we were together, throwing my empty beer cans into your empty fireplace, for nothing. That was preparation for this moment. And so was the time I spent with the IAEA freezing my arse off in Vienna.'

She said, 'As Stephen would say, the White Knight thing all began with the Arthurian legends and Gawain – all these series are about Round Table knights – it can never really be an old-wave idea.' She was referring to Stephen Knight, associate professor, a medievalist.

'*Through the Looking Glass* too,' he said, ' there is a White Knight in *Through the Looking Glass*. I re-read it during my hepatitis. Admittedly, a different sort of White Knight.'

Alice looked on with great interest as the King took an enormous memorandum-book out of his pocket, and began writing. A sudden thought struck her, and she took hold of the end of the pencil which came some way over his shoulder, and began writing for him.

The poor King looked puzzled and unhappy, and struggled with the pencil for some time without saying anything; but Alice was too strong for him, and at last he panted out, 'My dear!. . . it writes all manner of things that I don't intend -' . . . Alice had put 'The White Knight is sliding down the poker. He balances very badly.' The Queen said, 'That's not a memorandum of *your* feelings!'

Sandra said that she always felt a nausea sweep over her when she heard adults quoting Lewis Carroll. People clung to these books to make themselves oh-so-very-childlike and yet, at the same time, suggesting that they could grasp the enigma of existence from reading these books.

He said quickly that he had not touched a Lewis Carroll book for thirty years. 'It was during my hepatitis. I regressed.'

'All right then.'

'Hepatitis is a crisis of existential dimension - streets seem threatening and impenetrable. When the liver isn't working some fundamental harmony is shattered. That's what the *Village Voice* says. So you go back to books like Lewis Carroll.'

'You mustn't go on about your hepatitis. People with hepatitis seem to enjoy talking about it.'

'With hepatitis - well, suddenly, you know, that's all that's left.'

But it was agreed that he was to do a treatment for a White Knight series. Sandra suggested he talk with Laura Jones as a possible co-script writer. He made a file and wrote on it in Textacolour 'White Knight', and in brackets, '(ring Laura Jones)'.

Now, turning forty, it was good to know the next life move.

On November 21, he came into his work room with the morning newspapers and a coffee cup, a piece of toast and marmalade held dog-like in his mouth because his hands were full. He dropped the newspapers on the desk where they fell onto the folder saying, 'White Knight (ring Laura Jones)' in green Textacolour. As he watered the plants with a cup of cold undrunk coffee, there on his desk from last week, and wondered again if it did the plants harm, he tilted his head to read the newspaper lying on the desk and read '. . .had been planning a simultaneous suicide ceremony for months to be carried out if the code "White Knight" was broadcast by Leader Jones. . .'

He stopped watering or coffeeing the plants and sat down to read the newspaper with an alertness which became a chill.

AAP–Reuter –   : Georgetown : November 21. People's Temple members in Guyana and the United States had been planning a simultaneous suicide ceremony for months to be carried out if the code 'White Knight' was broadcast by Leader Jones.

The code apparently was not broadcast but Jones summoned his followers to the death meeting by telling them over the loudspeaker, 'The time has come for us to meet in another place.'

Although he had almost recovered from the hepatitis his body was still skewed by it, and it was with a residue of the sickness that he sat there in his swivel chair; even its slight motion gave his body a feeling of precariousness.

Shakily, he finished his toast and marmalade and read the report with a welling anxiety.   .

He very much doubted that he would begin work that morning on the White Knight series with Laura Jones – aura Jones – as co-script writer. No.

What would have happened to him had Jones broadcast the code White Knight? Should he stay indoors? Would that help? Was it better to move about?

And what sort of questions were these to be asking?

At the New Hellas lunch club that day, having done no work, he said to the political and historical people there at lunch that the Jonestown suicides must be the most bizarre post–Second World War news story 'and my own story is just as bizarre'.

He told them his story.

Donald said, 'So what? There is nothing to be said about it, even if it is the most bizarre news story of the post–Second World War period. And even if your story is equally bizarre, there is nothing to be said about it. It is an historical aberration. It says nothing about the United States that we don't already know – or about the West – it says nothing about the decline or fall of anything. That is often the case with aberrations of history.'

They all turned then to him, as a tennis crowd moves its head, looking to him to prove there was something perhaps to be said about it.

He found, as Donald claimed, that there was nothing really to be said.

'But there must be something to be said,' he came back. 'You people must have something to say. It could not be beyond analysis.'

'What then?'

'I don't know what. All I know is that I was in the fallout zone.'

Donald snorted.

They looked at him – the lunch club – with censure for having introduced a promising subject and for then having nothing to say. They went on to talk about the coming of the republic.

All right, there may be nothing to be said, he thought, nothing to be said there in the New Hellas about the Jonestown suicides, but it asks that something be said. Or was it saying something, not to the lunch club, or to the world, but to him alone.

In bed with Belle, his friend the slut, he said that he thought it was the most bizarre news story of the post-Second World War period. Maybe nothing like it has ever happened in recorded history, he said. And then added his own story.

'Is that not bizarre? Is there not a message in this for me?'

'I'd like to get some sleep now,' Belle said, hitting the pillow in emphatic preparation for sleep. 'Why don't you get decent pillows?'

'I was brought up to be able to sleep on anything,' he told her. He said 'Don Anderson' of the *Australian* bureau in New York says that it was probably the greatest mass suicide in history and I was nearly part of it. But I suspect a Jewish village in Poland might claim the record. There were, I believe, mass protest suicides among the Jews from time to time.'

'Go to sleep now,' she said, 'you mustn't let it preoccupy you. Your libido needs sleep even if you don't.'

'I can't help my libido – hepatitis affects the libido.'

'And turning forty.'

'Turning forty has nothing to do with it. I was actually quoting Knight to Sandra and he's an expert on the Knight's Tale from Chaucer. It all links up.'

'Mmmmm.'

Belle was not the right person for him to be with now he was forty. She claimed to be a representation of his great-grandmother, but that wasn't enough.

That was all right too.

At the Thanksgiving party put on by Sam and Jessie, Jessie being an American, he said to the gathering partygoers that the Jonestown suicides must be the most bizarre news story of the post–Second World War period, 'and I have a pretty bizarre story of my own to tell too – connected with it.'

The guests at the Thanksgiving listened thankfully to his story but he arrived at the end of the story to find that they had nothing to say.

'Imagine the poor stringer in Georgetown,' Jessie said, 'trying to convince the bureau in New York that four hundred Americans got together in the jungle and suicided.'

That was a contribution to the story but it was not the aspect upon which he wanted to focus attention.

Jessie said that the bureau probably told him, 'Go have another drink, Harry.'

'But what about Laura Jones – aura Jones?'

'In New York they probably said "jungle juice",' one of the party said.

'There must be something more to be said about it,' he prompted.

The Thanksgiving conversation could do nothing with it. Everyone became thoughtful.

'Surely things can't be that bad in the United States,' Jessie's father said, at last. He was visiting Australia. 'In our country, can things really be that bad?'

He waited for Jessie's father to say more. But no more was said. The conversation hung there among the thoughtful guests, but nothing more came.

As they all went in for their turkey and pumpkin pie, he said to Jessie's father that he wouldn't take it to mean the decline or fall of the West. Jessie's father said he hoped not.

In the car on the way to the airport to drop Louise, an ex–lover who was passing through on her way back to the United States where she worked in the UK Embassy, he said that he had planned a television series on his IAEA experience with the working title 'White Knight' taken from a lecture by Stephen Knight. He had intended to work on it with Laura Jones – aura Jones – and how on the first day of work the Jonestown suicides occurred according to the plan 'White Knight'. And how he'd been feeling rather suicidal himself.

'Is that a bad omen for the series,' he asked her, 'or is that a bad omen!'

'Or is it a bad omen for you. For you turning forty,' she said. 'Did you read that hepatitis can not only affect your libido but that it can take away your will to live?'

'I have no will to live. Never have had. I could hardly have not read it since you sent it to me marked with a Stabilo pen. And you shouldn't say things like that,' he said, 'to the sick.'

'You told me once that the sick, too, love truth,' she replied. 'And you have to make up your mind whether you take omens or whether you don't take omens. Now that you're forty.'

They kissed at customs control and he felt shielded by the automatic sliding doors of the airport departure tunnel and glad that she was out of the country – her and her Stabilo spells.

In December he turned forty. He spent Christmas and his birthday with Belle, the wrong person. They stayed drunk and debauched in motels around the country and then in the bush, but they knew they were the wrong people to spend birthdays and Christmases with and that they were waiting for someone more suitable to those sorts of occasions to come along in their lives.

'But it feels OK,' she said.

'Oh yes,' he said, with genuine enthusiasm.

In February he met his friend Milton at the international airport on his return from study leave in the US.

Milton said, first thing, 'What about the Jonestown suicides!'

'Why do you mention the Jonestown suicides?'

'I was in this commune in San Francisco when it all happened,' Milton said, who always spent his study leave in a commune. 'We were on the fringe of that scene.'

'Here, let me take your luggage,' he said to Milton, 'but go on, tell me about Jonestown and I'll tell you *my* story.'

'I had this incredible fight with Sheena – really bad in a way neither of us had before with anyone else in our lives or with each other. We generally never fight like that. Pulling hair – smashed mirrors – and she scratched me, flesh under her fingernails. . .'

'A White Knight private investigator would have found the flesh under the fingernails.'

'What?'

'Nothing – go on.'

'It was so bad. We both went off – I went to this bar to drink myself to death. I don't know where she went but we both felt suicidal. She tried to telephone this doctor she knew to get sleeping pills. I kept working out in the bar how to drink enough to kill myself. Next day: Jonestown.'

'Jonestown.'

'Yes, really! A guy at the commune who is into lasers said that the Jonestown thing triggered suicides all over the country. That there was this beaming out from Jonestown and Sheena and I were lucky to have resisted it – just. The signal was too weak.'

'It could have been the hills. The reception is bad in the hills of San Francisco.'

They put the luggage in the car.

'How was Jones going to broadcast the signal?' he asked Milton, who knew these things.

'It was a beam – a head beam.'

'Oh. I thought that it was Alice holding the end of the pen,' he told Milton, jocularly, 'that's our lives.'

'You're right!' Milton said. 'The CIA is in there somewhere.'

'I'll tell *you* my story.'

'Hold on,' said Milton, 'I'll tell you what's really coming down the tube from the Jonestown thing.'

Milton talked dysrhythmically as they drove around the car park looking for an exit. Milton hit his forehead with his hand, 'Of course – I missed at first – the Ballad of the White Knight – White Knight! Jesus the ramifications are fantastic.'

But he thought that Milton seemed to shrink away from him after he had told *his* story of the White Knight.

He did not work in January – the White Knight folder was still lying on his desk from November. When wandering in the city, hours early for an appointment, he bought the seamail *Economist* for November 25.

The *Economist* had 'something to say.'

The religious sects are the grass forcing itself through the concrete. . .religious innovation is one of the last and best examples of free enterprise. . .half forgotten fragments of animism and the dark other side of the religious coin. . .if things go well the time between now and the 21st century could prove to be as important in the development of human consciousness as, say, the fifth century BC (which saw orderly intellectual thought taking root in Greece); the first century of the Christian era (which saw the offering of a new link between the spiritual and material halves of life); the seventh century (which saw the first real explosion of the idea of man's individual powers and responsibilities). . .it could lead to a pacification of the long civil war in inner space. . .most appear to have drunk cyanide found mixed with grape drink in a tin tub. Mr Jones had dispensed mock suicide potions before. The spasms of the first children ended any doubt. Many tried to run into the jungle. They were turned back by the camp's armed guards or shot down. . .at one level the story is another example of the special quality of

America; the country where the best is better, but the worst is also worse, than anywhere on the globe.

The pacification of the long civil war in inner space, yet.

Now if the *Economist* leader writer had been at lunch at the New Hellas he would have had something to say. But it was not a Sydney way of talking. We could do with some panoramic thinkers.

AAP–Milton telephone, 'More on Jonestown – I'm over my dysrhythmia now – more stuff is coming down – I'm told there are 913 bodies in a hangar at Dover Air Force base in Delaware. No one will claim them. They will remain there forever. Refrigerated. A complete commune. The dead commune – the title's yours, have it, take it. The ramifications are truly fantastic.'

'It's the grass forcing itself through the concrete,' he told Milton.

'Riiiight!'

Was this the commune which beckoned him? Was this the commune, at last, which wanted him?

He learned from a friend in the US airforce that the bodies were in fact flown from Dover Air Force base to California to be buried. Delaware didn't want them buried there.

Sandra rang about the television treatment on the White Knight series and he told her he had not done any work on it. He told her why.

She said, 'Oh,' and then asked him how he was coping with being forty.

'Fine,' he said.

'Are you sure?'

In April, he read that the code name for the suicide pact was not 'White Knight' but 'White Night'. It had been misreported. There was no explanation of either code name.

He felt something lift from his whimpering psyche but still could not work on the White Knight project.

He rang Milton. 'They had it wrong,' he told him.

'But Jesus.' Milton said, 'you came within one letter of being hit by the laser.'

'I missed by one letter – a kay. I'm A–Okay.'

'Don't joke – that's the way it works. There's a lot of stuff coming out on that sort of thing from Hungary.'

That week while contemplating beginning work 'on the treatment' (and his new life) he fell down writhing with pain on the floor of his office amid the struggling indoor plants.

Gripped with agony, he called a taxi which took him to the doctor and from there he was taken to hospital for emergency surgery.

He came out of the operation with tubes in his mouth, nose, and penis, and with a drip in his arm.

They gave him Pentathol and he saw a sun-filled field of yellow flowers and it beckoned to him. It was, he thought, death beckoning. No doubt. He considered it, saw his great-grandmother and grandfather standing in the field beckoning, but for no obvious reason decided this time to say no he wouldn't go yet into the never-ending warmth of that sun and to death's corny field of swaying yellow flowers. Not yet.

He then fell into a deep sleep and did not die.

He convalesced on his own in a small quiet hotel. He could not go to Belle's house because she was not someone you convalesced with, her life-urge was over-vigorous, and she had once said that she was 'into scars'.

The months of August and September he spent in Canberra, the seat of government, on IAEA business. While in that city a Senator Knight rang and wanted to talk to him about nuclear waste.

Of all the senators why Senator Knight? He told himself that it was White *Night* now that he had to watch – the Knight business was all over. But he went to the appointment cautiously.

Nothing of note occurred.

In August, still in Canberra, he read a poem in the magazine *Quadrant* written by Evan Jones. He did not register the name Jones until he had entered the poem.

Sometimes he read poems because he knew the poet, sometimes because of the title, sometimes he just grabbed a poem and read it as a random sample of 'poetry being written now'. He had read this poem as such a sample.

It was titled *Insomniacs* but he was not an insomniac, that was not the reason he read the poem.

In stanza three he read:

Insomniacs, bless them, are never afraid of the dark:
bad nights are called 'white nights' for that dull white
which lurks behind their eye-lids, dingy, mean.
Nothing at all like innocence, purity or peace,
signalling that all the nerves would like to break.
Something in the whole being is at war.

He put down the magazine. Oh oh, something was still going on. The laser was still searching for him.

That night and for a few nights he sweated after going to bed, fearing that his sleep would now be disrupted   -   that that had been the message of the poem. Could you die from sleep deprivation?

His two companions in Canberra were named Lewis and after a heavy drinking bout with one of the Lewises, in the week he read the poem, he became ill again with hepatitis.

He could hardly move from his bed, pinned down with an immense lethargy. He found that he could now do nothing else *but sleep*.

It had got him, the laser.

That night while lying in bed with his new sickness in his rooms at University House he heard music from a radio carried on the wind and he heard the announcer say that the piece of music which had reached him on the wind was called *White Night* and that it was played by Kenny White and his orchestra. The wind dropped and he heard no more.

While lying there during the next few days he wondered why his two companions in that city   -   the seat of government   -   should both be named Lewis. He asked one and she said that Cottle's Dictionary of Surnames said that Lewis meant 'great battle'.

'Why do you ask?'

He shook his head, the message was there but could not be shared.

This Lewis dropped in the airmail *Guardian* to him to read and he read that the Moscow International Book Fair had refused to allow the book *White Nights* by Israel's Prime Minister Mr Begin to enter the Soviet Union. The book was an account of Begin's persecution and torment in a Soviet labour camp.

In the next airmail *Guardian* he read of a recent screening of Bresson's *Four Nights* which was based on Dostoyevsky's story *White Nights* and he further read that Visconti also had made a film called *White Nights* based on the Dostoyevsky story.

Hepatitis had drained his energy so that clipping even the tissue-thin pages of the airmail *Guardian* took a long time, but he clipped the two reports and would, from time to time, study them for messages.

The clippings yielded nothing but the word 'guardian' addressed itself to him and he felt comforted by it.

There was, he intuited, an airmail or air-male or heir-male Force of Destruction coming in from around Jonestown and an heir-male Guardian. There was a battle going on for his psyche. He being, of course, the male heir. His suicidal grandfather was mixed up in it somewhere.

As soon as he was well enough he went to the National University library and found all Dostoyevsky's work there except *White Nights*.

He stood there in the gloomy aisles of books sweating from a nervous impotence, having confirmed, once again, that desperate feeling he always had in libraries that what he wanted would not be there, or that he was looking in the wrong place.

'What does it mean that the book *White Nights* by Dostoyevsky is not in the library?' he asked a helpful, new-breed librarian in jeans.

'It could be out on loan.'

He wanted a different category of answer to his questions. But that was asking too much even from a new-breed librarian.

'But all his other books are there in multiple copies.'

'Maybe it is at the binder – that would be another possibility.'

'That all the copies of *White Nights* wore out at the same time? Could you check to see who has all the copies of *White Nights*?'

'That would be confidential. Would you like it to be public knowledge that you, say, borrowed a book on menopause, hypothetically – if you were a woman?'

He did not wish to be drawn into hypothetical discussion – in another gender – on menopause.

'It's odd that's all,' he said, a touch of peevishness in his voice, 'that you have multiple copies of all of Dostoyevsky's work but that all the copies of that title alone are missing.'

She shrugged, and began to fidget nervously with her confidential cards, moving surreptitiously towards the security button.

'Never mind,' he said.

'You're welcome.'

He had never been welcome, not for one day on this planet had he ever felt welcome.

Outside the library, he thought, I am becoming grumpy, I am now forty and I am becoming grumpy.

He recovered and returned to his own city where he told Belle about the *White Nights* and about the books missing from the library and the rest.

'That's odd,' she said, humouring him.

'Don't humour me,' he said, grumpily, 'I think it bears some attention.'

'I cannot explain the *White Nights* thing,' she said, watching him, he thought, closely, 'but I have two copies of Dostoyevsky's *White Nights*, but I don't want you to make anything of it.'

'Why two copies of Dostoyevsky's *White Nights*?'

'I cannot explain why I have two copies and I do not want you to make a thing of it.'

She brought him a copy of the book.

He examined it and read the novella *White Nights*.

He then explained to Belle that white night referred to the midsummer nights at the sixtieth latitude north.

'So?'

'I am in the midsummer latitude of my life.'

'Oh.'

In November, one year from the Jonestown suicides, an American journalist flew in and telephoned him, Joe Treaster from the *New York Times*.

Joe Treaster wanted to talk to him about the IAEA.

'Who put you on to me?'

'The Department of Information.'

A few days later a friend rang and invited him to a party. 'Joe Treaster from the *New York Times* will be there. You should meet him.'

'Yes, he rang me.'

'Did you know he was the first journalist into Jonestown after the suicides? He's very interesting on it.'

'No!'

He then rang Joe at his hotel but could not reach him and left a message for Joe to ring back.

But he was due in Vienna and could not fit in with Joe's itinerary. They didn't meet, which he thought was probably just as well.

That week Senator Knight from Canberra dropped dead at the age of forty.

He gave up the *White Knight* TV project, not having written a word of it.

He said to Belle that he did not really suffer from the illusion that the universe was rearranging itself to give him a personal message. He knew that was ultimate egoism.

But he could be excused for thinking it was a year of shadows, confusing linguistic signals, ricocheting beams, that maybe a bony hand had been groping for him, inviting him to dance, lanterns had been waved in the dark to guide him towards the cliff. But he was through it now.

'That's a relief,' Belle said, 'I thought for a while there you were loony tunes.'

Later in the next year, having again given up the idea of being a writer, he was working at a university and they had given him a room formerly occupied by a medievalist.

He was seated at the desk for some hours before he realised that a poster of an ivory chess piece on the wall facing him was a white knight – the caption said it was from the Isle of Lewis. The white knight was glum and toy–like and it did not frighten him. He photographed it and during his time at the university became quite fond of it.

• LIBIDO AND LIFE LESSONS •

When he noticed that his libido was low while in Vienna the first time he thought it was because he was travelling – the beast out of its habitat does not feel secure enough to mate or, maybe, to perform any part of the breeding act. He reasoned that animals needed to be confident of their safety. But we are not purely animals. And sometimes he had become randy while travelling. Now he didn't feel randy for days and days. It continued after his return to Australia.

'Hullo,' he said, 'is this some sort of suicide?' Was this why his grandfather committed suicide? Which came first, the loss of interest in life or the loss of libido?

His fantasy life became dulled. He was able to have sex, but without much drive. Another explanation was that he was 'growing up' and putting behind him random sexuality. Was this the way an adult genital male should be at forty? All the books said that turning forty should not affect the libido. Were the books lying?

He found too that he desired to *feel desire* as much as he wanted to have sex; to feel the full juices of desire, to be restless with appetite would please him now.

He could recall the visitations of desire for Belle. The desire strong enough to make him get up from his bed into a car and to drive in the middle of the night to see her.

He understood why Faust in the Gounod opera wanted the return of desire as part of his contract with the devil.

Or was he in fact better off without it?

He wondered if it were absent long enough would it fade as a known part of his person – would the feel of it be beyond imaginative recall, even?

That might be all right.

It was, he would now have to explain to Belle, that he could still visually recognise sensuality or sexual attractiveness but it seemed disconnected from the hormonal physical reaction in him. The line was down.

It then occurred to him that it might be related to his hepatitis attack.

His liver specialist was bemused by the question. 'Yes, but I am a *liver* specialist.'

The doctor pondered it. 'It is possible that the liver which controls the flow of oestrogen into the body and out of the body could be affected by hepatitis. Maybe an over-supply of oestrogen.'

His meeting with Belle, the self-proclaimed slut of all times, confirmed that his libido was ailing. Her allure no longer called to him across great distances, and desire for her no longer fell upon him like a fully armed woman jumping from a tree.

'What is up with you?' she said, after they'd finished a rather underpowered lovemaking.

'I'm not full on,' he said.

'I can tell that.'

'I'm suffering from an over-supply of oestrogen. From my hepatitis.'

'You're turning into a woman?'

'No, not quite.'

'You were erect but you lacked a certain follow-through, a certain zing.'

'Maybe it's turning forty. Maybe the books lie. It's cruel.'

'Oh come on – if it's from your hepatitis it'll pass. But tell me, what is being forty "like"?'

He told Belle what being forty is 'like'.

You finally accept that you cannot drink a cup of hot take-away coffee and drive a car at the same time.

You doubt that you will ever go to a 'party' again. Parties cease to be events of unlimited possibility.

You realise that you have spent forty years raising the child within you.

You find your ex-wife dying of cancer, that another friend has a noticeable lump on his face but you do not refer to it.

You read your CV with a comfortable curiosity to find out 'what you really are.' You run through your credentials and life experiences to remind yourself that you have 'fully lived'. You find yourself sitting in a bar reading your passport reminding yourself of the world you've seen, about which you seem to recall so little.

You have a feeling that it's too late to bother a psychiatrist with your problems, too late to reconstruct yourself, that you have now to *live it out*. And you have a feeling that a psychiatrist wouldn't think it worth wasting time on you – too little life left to live usefully.

You have an urge to close up your life for a year and go to the seaside and re-read all the important books of your life; feeling that maybe you didn't read them properly when younger or that you would 'get more from them' now. Or that you have forgotten too much of them.

You find that expressions like 'doing what you like' and 'being nice to yourself' are traps which answer nothing very much. Respite can only follow volatility of human interaction, stress and friction are part of life, and anxiety a fairly predictable background to a dangerous and uncertain world.

The excesses of life are too easily achieved, are not heroic, and yield less and less. You realise that the better pleasures are 'managed', structured, carefully sculptured from a won life.

The past becomes closer, as you yourself have a history. Being forty gives you an understanding of what 'forty years' is in time, how close that is. Something that happened say fifty years before you were born becomes dramatically closer.

You see sleep as 'part of life', not time wasted or something you 'do too much of'. You learn to enjoy sleep. You see your dreams as an interesting part of living.

You realise the huge distance between written descriptions of biographical detail and the density of conflict and despair which lies in the minutes and hours of those biographical descriptions. That success is always disputed, qualified by self-doubt and challenged by the ever-changing hierarchy of following generations. The formal moments and rewards of success usually come after the desire for those formal moments and rewards has passed.

You have days where the repetition of nail-cutting, hair-cutting, teeth-cleaning, arse-wiping, and the ever-present deterioration of self and the material world about you, tires you beyond belief.

You still sometimes hope for a dramatic opening in your life, for your life to alter course after meeting someone, after receiving a letter. You sometimes wish to feel the dramatic upheaval, renovation and certainty of blind conversion.

You realise that you've never really got your life together. That there are parts of your life always in disarray, things not properly completed, living arrangements which could be improved, life practices which could be improved. You feel at times that you need to delimit your life so as to live a more reduced life more perfectly.

You notice that fragments of past night dreams, fragments of travel, inconsequential fragments of past relationships, childhood, begin to intrude or drift across your consciousness with no discernible pattern or meaning, perhaps with an intimation of insanity, derangement.

You realise that you have been 'homeless' most of your life, living in other people's houses, in camps, in motels, in hotels. You have camped in life.

With regret you realise that no person with a system of knowledge is going to release you from intellectual dilemma. No book will now come along to seriously alter your life. You feel that you have a fair grasp of the current limitations of knowledge and reason, and the necessary, compromising uses of faith. You recognise that your personal, unstable formulations are held without much confidence to stave off the sands of chaotic reality, that a refinement might take their place but you also fear that the rational shoring might one day give way entirely. You are daily made aware of how little reason and knowledge altered the course of affairs.

After coming to terms with the imperfect self it is then necessary to come to terms with the imperfect world, to calculate how much of the imperfection of self and the world you have to accommodate without restlessness, without engaging in ineffective efforts to change, efforts which are more protest and despair than hoped-for interventions. What parts to find unacceptable, to bewail, to retaliate against. How much evil to live with. How much mess. To calculate the 'unchangeable'.

As well as the demands of being a loving person, from which you constantly fall short, you have to live with recrudescence of love for lovers lost, who come alive unannounced in your mind, dreams. Call to you. You find you cry over spilt love.

You learn that most things require a proper time for their performance for the thing to be savoured, to be performed with gratification. Including shopping.

You strive to keep all conversations exploratory and all positions negotiable and to avoid people who push conversation into competitiveness, or make you insecure or over-defensive, or cause you to perform poorly intellectually. Some people jam your mind and lower its quality of performance. Some people raise this performance.

You realise that nothing is really forgotten or lost to the mind, simply that access to the memory bank became erratic.

You read reports and letters written many years before and realise that you'd known much that you no longer consciously know. You hope that it is working for you in your chain of reasoning which stretched back twenty-five years.

The secret of negotiation is to break the deal into many smaller, tradeable parts.

You wonder if omens are unconsciously formed patterns made from myriad inputs and then erupting as signals, warnings, cautions, guidelines, messages – self-planted, self-addressed, but given this form for urgent dramatic revelation.

You are unable to determine whether you have led the richest of lives or the most miserable and deformed of lives.

'Well,' Belle said, 'is that all? Is that all you've learned?'

'What is sad,' he said, 'is that I've learned some of these things more than once.'

'I think I'll wait until I have to learn some of those lessons,' she said.

'Oh they come along in time, when they are no longer of much use.'

• DELEGATE •

It was at the Kunsthistorisches Museum in Vienna that he first glimpsed the face of his seventeen-year-old girlfriend in the face of his seventy-year-old co-delegate, Edith.

The face of his seventeen year-old appeared through the distortion of the double glass of a showcase there in the museum. The distortion came from seeing through both sides of the glass case, the angle of vision too maybe - and maybe the aura of the liturgical objects or whatever, who knows? - this together with his yearning for his girlfriend, all went to create her face, perfectly but fleetingly. Edith then moved and came around the other side of the showcase and her face returned to being that of the seventy-year-old and the girl was gone.

'Go back around the other side of the case, Edith,' he asked, prepared though for the illusion to be exposed the second time around.

'Why?' she asked, going back at his bidding anyhow. 'Here?'

He bent down again and squinted at her through the double glass, but it was no good. Something wasn't there.

'How long must I remain here?' she asked.

'It's all right, that's it.'

'What was all that about?' she asked, coming back to where he was.

'There was an optical distortion,' he said, 'it pleased me. I could see you as a young girl – you looked very girlish.'

'Would that one could always move, then, in a glass showcase.'

'I think it was the magic coming off. . .' he glanced at the label in the showcase, 'the second–century glass liturgical vessel.'

They moved listlessly through the museum. He stared unseeingly at the objects, the other floors had dazzled him into apathy. Edith tried to make notes which would keep all that she was seeing and half-seeing fresh and organised in her crowded mind.

In this his fortieth year he had planned to visit Spain with the young girl – well, she was no longer seventeen, except in a master frozen frame of his multiple visions of her. But she had 'fallen in love' and was unable to make the trip with him. Instead he found himself as one of the team at the IAEA General Conference along with Edith.

At the beginning of her Grand Tour the girl had written, 'I wish you were here with your hip flask of brandy and crooked talk.' But a second card had come, 'I have fallen in love.'

He wished so badly that she was there with him in Vienna with her carefully worded assertions, her nicely judged quotations, all so newly won from her thinking and study – and he yearned for the physical intoxication she could bring to him.

'You seem glum,' Edith said.

'Too much history. Human race too old.'

At breakfast without his glasses he was again pierced by the young girl's image crossing Edith's old face as she entered the breakfast room after a night's rest. But as she came into focus, the suggestion of the girl went and it was the seventy–year–old who sat down.

Edith went straight into the jam, cold cuts and cheese. She had a youthful appetite.

He too began to eat. Why was it that in Austria he enjoyed the Austrian breakfast, in the US the US breakfast, in France the French breakfast, yet back home he didn't eat breakfast?

He asked Edith whether she had a theory about it.

'No. . .' she said, wary of his teasing, 'no, I have no theory on that.' And then she added, 'That I know of.'

'Changes of habitat require different diets. Maybe we're symbolically eating the prey of the country we're in.'

'Cheese?'

She wasn't going to be led into jokey ground.

'Sleep well, Edith?'

'No, as a matter of fact, I had a restless night – I could hear strange water noises,' she said, taking a mouthful of roll and jam, 'Yourself?'

'Oh yes, I slept well, I'm a bushman – a few cognacs and all noises sound friendly.'

'You would be the first bushman I've known who drank cognac. I might ask for a different room – would they mind?'

'Of course not – but the hotel is probably full. Delegations and staff.'

'I think I shall, though.'

'See Frau Smidt.'

'I think I shall. Or do you think I should see someone from the Embassy?'

'No, see Frau Smidt.'

She spread more blackcurrant jam on her roll, taking his share of the sachets.

'You don't think I should also tell the Embassy. . .'

'No.' He held back his impatience, 'There's no need.'

She exasperated him. He scrounged another mouthful from the dwindling breakfast food and waited for what he knew would be her request. He knew it was coming.

'Would you mind dreadfully asking her for me – your German is so much better than mine.'

'Edith – you know I have very little German. Her English is fine. But yes, I'll ask for you.'

'Thanks awfully, I can't cope with that sort of thing, I know I'm being silly. . .these days women should, I know. . .try.'

She made this admission without conviction and at the same time poured the coffee pot dry.

He studied Edith while they sat in the auditorium listening to instantaneous translation of the speaker through headphones, an African stating that nuclear war fears were 'Western hysteria'.

He ached to see the face of his young girlfriend appear in Edith's face again, but it would not. He moved his seat, he half-closed his eyes to reduce the light, he pulled the skin near the eyes with his fingers to cause distortion in his sight, but nothing brought back the girl's face. Edith's worried face remained as she strained to follow the argument and as she made frowns of satisfaction and wallowed in being appalled.

She liked being appalled. He suspected it was her strongest emotion.

In his room at the Hotel Stephanplatz he drank cognac and read Goethe's *Faust*, stalling now and then with self-consciousness, recalling the Consul in *Under the Volcano*, who also read *Faust* and drank – though he'd read Marlowe's *Faust*. Marlowe was next on the reading list. But given the Germanic influence about him and their mission, what else?

He hadn't been able to face the evening session of Non-government Organisations – too much piety and youthful attempts at re-invention of the world.

Age is an ague fever, it is clear / with chills of moody want and dread; When one has passed his thirtieth year, / One then is just the same as dead [says Baccalaureus, the young student. . .Mephistopheles replies] My children, it may be so; / Consider now, the Devil's old; to understand him, be also old!

He guessed that Edith would be back from the evening session and he went to her room, wanting company, even Edith's limited company. It was 11.35 p.m., at least politely before midnight. He knocked. Was he drunk?

'Yes, who is it?' she called, from behind the door.

'It's me.'

She came to the door in a robe over her slip. She looked very old, identified by dress with her generation now passing out of life. But he felt, despite her age, that she still didn't 'know the devil'.

'I was preparing for bed – you wanted something?'

Then. For an instant. Their eyes met in a weak glow of sought desire – like a torch with failing batteries – but this was extinguished instantly as he recoiled with the physical incompatibility of it. The utter unfeasibility of it. He was sure she had registered it but she looked away, nervously erasing whatever faint carnal sensation she had picked up, or, sent out.

He'd wanted, he realised, then, to glimpse the girl, moved by a foggy concupiscence, a dim, unformed intention of somehow lurchingly imposing his erotic exigence on her aged body, but even in the dim night lights of the hotel corridor the girl was not there. Even with so much cognac twisting his imagination, he could not find the girl there in her.

'I thought you might have a spare airmail letter form – the late-night letter-writing – from the darkness of the soul.'

She was flustered and left him standing at the door while she went to look.

She stopped half-way across her room and turned back to him. 'An airmail letter form?'

'Yes, just one.'

She turned away and then turned back again. 'Oh do come in – how rude of me – I'm getting ready for bed.'

'Is the room quieter?' he asked, as he came in and stood in the middle of the room.

'Yes, thanks awfully, it was decent of you to arrange it all.'

He saw her medicines beside her bed. Medicines of ageing.

She handed him the airmail form and he left.

Down the corridor he stopped. He wanted to look at her once more, to try once more to see his girl's face in her. He retraced his steps to her door and tried it, found it still unlocked, and opened it, without premeditation.

He was in the room and Edith was standing naked and shocked.

He thought of a skinned kangaroo and then mumbled, 'Sorry,' and went back out the door, closing it behind him.

Mephistopheles: I thought to meet with strangers here! / And find my relatives, I fear: / But, as the ancient scriptures tell us, the world is kin, from Hartz to Hellas. / I've many forms, in action swift, / For transformation is my gift / But in your honour, be it said. . . / I have put on my ass's head. . . / Faust: caste one by one your maskes aside! / and lay your hideous nature bare! / . . .My choice is made: this pretty dear. . . / Alas, dry broom sticks have I heare / . . . this little darling would I clasp . . . / A lizard wriggles from my grasp.

At the early breakfast before the trip to the contemporary art exhibition he said good morning to the Canadians, *bon jour* to the Cameroons, *guten morgen* to the waitress, and made his way to where Edith was already seated, eating her way through the rolls, jams, meats and cheeses. He decided to ignore the embarrassment of the night before.

'The Austrian idea of a rest day,' he said, 'up an hour earlier than usual to be bussed out of the city.'

He avoided her eyes, as a guilty dog. But she spoke brightly to convey to him, he thought, that nothing was amiss, all was to go on as before.

She stayed with him throughout the visit to the art exhibition although he tried to disengage from her, to be apart from her for a time. But she'd said, plaintively, 'Would you mind if I clung on to you? – I'm feeling a little off today.'

He realised that she was exploiting his impropriety of the night before, taking a compensatory payment.

As they moved around the galleries together, she would say, 'But is this really art?' She'd been happier at the Kunsthistorisches.

After a while he said to her, 'I suppose art is what you find in art galleries.'

Some of the material was displayed in the Orangerie of the old summer palace and, while looking at this, Edith said, 'Maybe then, this isn't art but oranges we're looking at.'

He turned to her smiling, it was her first joke with him. 'Very good, Edith.' he said.

They stopped at photographs of the OM Theatre.

'Art or oranges?' became a running joke with them.

'Orgies and mysteries,' he said, reading from the programme notes. Edith peered, uncomprehendingly, at the photographs.

'You're looking at the entrails of a freshly slaughtered cow.'

She screwed up her face and with delight he saw again the girl's face, his girl was there again in the subdued lighting of the gallery, but it came too from the frowning face of puzzlement and the resistance to what she was seeing.

She stepped back and the girl was gone but she said, this time mocking herself, 'Is that really an orange? Or are we in the Orgierie now?'

He was trying to hold to the image of his girl, even though it was accompanied by the hurt of separation, but Edith's humour interfered with his privacy and he let it go.

After the opening of the exhibition the director, R.H. Luchs, said that the older artists should not pursue the splendid rashness of youth. To desire only the new and the young was a state of mind which bred nervousness and distorted one's personal history.

Sure did.

• • •

At breakfast back at the Hotel Stephanplatz he asked her.

'Edith, there's something I want to ask of you - a favour.'

'Of course - you've done lots of things for me on this trip - you've been really very considerate.'

'This is an unusual request - outside the boundaries of our mission.'

'Well, you can but ask.'

'There is a girl in London - I need her address and telephone number - I've lost contact.'

'And?'

'I want you to help me get the telephone number. She won't give it to me.'

He looked at her defencelessly.

'Where do I come into it? - it's rather odd - if indeed I do come into it,' her voice guarded.

'You could telephone her home in Adelaide - and ask for it - you could say - this is a cover story - that you found her wallet here in Vienna and wish to return it to her - you could say that's where you found her home address - in the wallet. Something like that.'

She sat silently, eating. Her hand trembled a little.

'By "cover story" you mean "lie",' she said, 'I'm not sure I could carry that off - or that I should. Never any good at lying.'

'Come on Edith - you've been in intrigues before surely - lovers' intrigues.'

She paused and thought. He hoped that 'lovers' intrigues' made it sound more acceptable. A small smile came to her face.

'But I'm a grandmother now. . .not an accomplice of. . .' Her words petered out.

'And you're a poet too.'

'Pshaw - one small book many years ago, which I may add has received more attention than it deserves, and what has that to do with anything?'

'Poets are. . .' With a gesture he gave the occupation of poet its traditional alliance with love. 'Poets are traditionally in alliance with lovers.'

'I suppose there is a small part of me which is still the poet. Aren't you a little old for these games?' He pretended to wince.

'Point taken - but she's young and I'm obliged to play them, it's her world I wish to belong to.'

'Although it surprises me,' she said, carefully, wiping the crumbs of bread roll from her mouth, frowning, 'and I don't know how to say it, and maybe I shouldn't say it, but I will – I don't know that I don't feel a little jealous.' She then smiled, embarrassedly. 'After all, you are my consort on this trip – in a way of speaking. Please excuse the double negatives.'

He raised an eyebrow, caught by this unexpected declaration, claim, or whatever. He leaned across, touched her old hand, 'Edith I am your consort.'

They both gave a little laugh at their declarations. Declarations of a valueless intimacy.

'Let me think about it then,' she said.

The Cameroons invited him to breakfast. They spoke English and expressed pleasure at his speech given at one of the unofficial functions. He felt irritated by guilt in the breakfast room because he was aware of Edith sitting at the other table on her own, not looking at them in a deliberate way. He absolutely rejected the guilt.

The Cameroons laughed about the behaviour of the German chair the night before. They seemed to have a taste for conference mischief-making. They laughed also about the work of Jonathan Schell and shook their heads about his thesis which had been often referred to.

'It could have been written only by an affluent American living in a leafy street with a swinging settee on the porch,' one of them said.

One of them said something in French and they giggled.

Dr Kum'a Ndumbe then gestured at them to stop, 'Enough giggling about Mr Schell.' He turned to him, 'You are from your government?'

'In a sense, yes, I carry a green passport – but not a red passport.'

'We thought perhaps there should be closer links between our countries – I don't have good reasons for this – it is purely impulsive.'

He agreed. He listened to Dr Kum'a Ndumbe talk and drifted into a fantasy about the Cameroons – maybe they had their fantasies about Australia, beef steaks, good dentistry, golden beaches.

His fantasy was to flee to another life for good. He called it his Mexican Feeling. He realised as he sat there in the Austrian hotel, playing this fantasy, that it didn't involve the girl. It was a flight from all known connections.

Outside Hermosillo once he had waited for a train, having been

warned to be 'early' for Mexican trains. He had arrived with hours to
wait. In a nearby bar he'd drunk with some comradely Mexicans.
When they left the bar some drinks later they'd invited him to go with
them, 'Come amigo, come with us.' He'd gone out of the dark bar
into the sunshine and looked to where they gestured, up the hill about
five kilometres away to a mud village sculptured into the hillside at
the end of a rough track. He could see smoke curling from the
chimneys, he could see the goats. The Mexicans had bought some
tequila and they said, 'Come with us, amigo – we'll eat and drink
some more. Mucho talk, mucho drink, mucho musica.' He looked
away up to their village and felt the hot sun and the creeping
relaxation of the alcohol.

If I go up to that village, he thought, I shall stay there.

He looked to his top-opening leather travelling bag with affection.
It was all he needed. Pick it up and go with the Mexicans. To reduce
his world to that one good old bag with the brass buckles.

One day a private detective sent by his relatives would come to the
village and show his photograph but he would not be recognised and
the village would protect his secret.

They would gather around the private detective saying, 'No
hombre, nix. No.'

Sitting now in the cool Austrian hotel talking with the Cameroons
he could feel the Mexican sun again and could taste again the Mexican
Bohemia beer, he could see the beckoning village, smell the goats.

'Come amigo, Mister Kangaroo, we'll eat and drink. Musico.'

Maybe he would marry one of their sisters – they could live well
on his Australian income even after he had been filed away as
'missing' in the Department.

'Si, musico, tequila.'

'No, el tren, mucho gracias,' he said, smiling wistfully, clapping
them on the back, 'mucho gracias. Another time.'

There in the Hotel Stephanplatz, Dr Kum'a Ndumbe talked of
scientific and cultural exchange. He would go to the Cameroons and
live high in the mountains amid the occasional cries of unidentified
brilliantly coloured birds and the occasional growl of a wild cat, and
at night, the incessant talking of the village drums, the village singing.
Cold gins and tonic. Ice? He came back then to the breakfast room of
the Stephanplatz to see a miffed Edith leaving the room without
gesturing or speaking.

• • •

He made it up to her by taking her to see some Max Ernst paintings, thinking that he wasn't required to 'make' anything up.

'Max Ernst's father painted a picture of his garden and left out the bough of a tree which he considered spoiled the symmetry of his painting. When he completed the painting he went and cut the bough from the tree to make the garden conform to the painting.'

Edith said that Ernst's paintings struck terror in her.

'He's really too strong for me,' she said, 'too many bad dreams in his paintings.'

'Ernst used what he called "optical provocateurs" to produce his visions.'

'Oh.'

'Yes, he manipulated his eyesight and field of vision to cause new images to appear to him.'

'I should have thought the world strange enough as it is without resorting to distortion.'

'. . .Yes, by fortunate accident. I found it at the airport. I too am an Australian which makes it all the more remarkable. Instead of taking it to the Embassy I thought I'd make direct contact — your name and number are in the back of the passport as next of kin.'

He could not hear the replies Edith was getting from the voice back in Australia.

'. . .Yes, in the ladies room at the airport. Very fortunate. Yes.'

He saw Edith write down an address and telephone number in the UK.

She finished up the call.

'I don't mind saying that I feel guilty about having done this.' she said turning to him, 'I don't feel good about it at all. And they will eventually find you out. And me. Obviously the girl does not want to communicate with you and perhaps you should respect that. But I suppose it is all too late now.'

'Sometimes you're quite formal, Edith.'

He stared at the address trying to decode what it meant about her life arrangements. A good part of London. A college? An apartment? Youth hostel? Squat?'

'Thank you Edith — you're a good sport. A messenger of Eros.'

She made a dismissive noise but was pleased with herself.

'I can only hope that it brings you joy.'

'I doubt it.'

'I'm so glad that all this sort of thing is behind me.'

He looked up from the address at her with curiosity. 'Is it really – all behind you?'

He had sometimes thought about when 'it' might all stop.

'Well,' she said, almost coyly, 'almost. Allow me some illusion.'

'I thought that now at forty, I wouldn't be vulnerable. I am.'

But to himself he couldn't define what it was he wanted from this girl.

'Oh the forties – they are the desperate years.'

She went to the window and seemed to be watching her past in procession out there in Stephanplatz.

She said, 'Oh, things are still glimpsed but the exhausting ardour is gone.'

She turned, 'I do hope that it brings you some joy.' Her voice quavered.

He thought how the attachments of travelling mimicked in some ways the attachments of domesticity, replicated an emotional attachment.

She moved and sat at her writing table and began to fiddle with papers, put on her reading glasses, acts of termination.

'You are a splendid consort and travelling companion, Edith.'

It was a little more than he felt but it was a payment of gratitude, and as he said it he also realised that it was on the way to becoming true. He was liking her.

She didn't say anything at first, busying herself with her papers, but she coloured a little and then did say, 'Thank you – be off now you silly boy and play your games – I know you must want to ring that illicitly obtained telephone number.' She waved him away.

He brooded about ringing the girl's number in London now that he had it. Almost certainly she was still 'in love' and still did not wish to communicate with him.

He was not obsessed with her in an operatic sense. He told himself. Firmly. She did however visit him daily as a recollection or when something appeared in his life which he wanted to share with her, when he wanted to try to explain things to her and by so doing, explain them to himself, and to give her gifts and to accept her gifts. She quietly insinuated herself into his mind when he was making love and at other times he conjured her to his mind when making love. The more he thought about it the more he felt he could make her an offer to compete with 'being in love', offer her feelings superior to it, with two or three cognacs he could successfully argue that what he offered

her was of value at least equal to that of 'being in love'. Which state
would he choose now at his age if offered? The romantic had lost its
dazzle. Or was he fooling himself? Did he really want to see the girl
again to be smitten with passion?

He rang her.

'How in fuck's name did you get my number!?'

'By detective work.'

'No – how? It's important. You were not supposed to get in
touch with me.'

'I got it. Ardour.'

'Crap. Did my brother give it to you? The weak shit.'

'I got it. But I take it you're not overjoyed to hear my voice and that
you are presumably still "in love"?'

'Yes. But I don't mind hearing your voice. Now that it's done.'

'And you won't be coming on our Great Expedition to Spain and
our homage to the Spanish anarchists?'

'No, I'm afraid not. No.'

'Are you all right?'

'Yes – why shouldn't I be?'

'If you come I promise you a great time.'

'You always gave me great times.'

'You sound changed.'

'I have changed – you haven't seen me for two years.'

'That's true.'

'I'm no longer your archetypal Young Girl. I'm all grown up now.'

'I know that.' Did he know that?

'Grown up and worse.'

'You weren't bad to begin with,' he laughed.

There was a silence. 'Or how do you mean "worse"?'

'I'm a world-travelled young woman now. I'm no longer so fresh
and innocent. We should leave what we had as something quite nice.'

' "Quite nice"?'

'Yes, it was quite nice the way things were. But I'm, well, not like
that now.'

He sensed then she had more to tell, wanted to be pursued with
questions.

'Why are you not "like that anymore"? I know you're "in love",
that's fine, that's quite OK.'

'No, I don't mean that. I'm not the same girl. I'm older. I'm

definitely not the sweet young girl. I'm older than I should be.' She
gave a laugh which was amused - at his expense - but with a
regretful ending - at her own expense.

'Have you been through some sort of tribulation?'

'You could call it that.'

'Stop being mysterious.'

Amputation? Drugs?

'As they say - "a girl has to eat".'

'Oh.'

'Well, don't sound surprised. I used to think you were inducting me
into it.'

'How so!?'

'All those expensive hotels, clothes you bought me when I was just a
teenager - gifts. You showed me how it all worked.'

He decided to let that statement cool.

'Why don't you go home, go back to Australia? I'll send you
money.'

'So that I work for you exclusively,' she laughed.

'I didn't mean it that way,' he said faintly.

'Why should I go home? I like London. I like it over here. You
taught me the good life. And you taught me. . .' again she laughed, the
same laugh, at both their expense, 'about pleasing older men. I may
be less romantic now but I sure am more proficient.'

He had trouble receiving this statement. 'I'm not an older man. In
the stereotyped sense. And I find this a little erotic.' He was trying not
to react morally, to not show dismay, to be light, urbane.

'I would have expected a more interesting response from you.'

That hurt.

'My more complicated reactions will follow. How about your
boyfriend - the one you're "in love with"?'

She gave her hard-edged laugh.

'Your voice sounds odd all of a sudden,' she said acutely, 'oh, he'll
be home soon and he won't be happy if he finds me talking to you.
That I know.'

'What does he think. . .about what you're doing?'

' "Whoring" is the word you're looking for. Naturally he enjoys it.
He's full of whore-fantasy shit too.' She laughed, 'But in his case it's
no fantasy. And he likes the money. And he doesn't suffer from
having a higher education or a higher sensibility.'

'I want to see you. Maybe we could have a drink. A martini. Paris?
London? I'm coming through that way.'

'No. Let's just say goodbye for now.'

'Please. Surely a social drink isn't too much to ask?'

That was a subterfuge. He didn't want only a social drink. He couldn't have settled just for that. She was a fire in his mind.

She added, 'Maybe sometime in the future.' And then said, 'You turned away from me once.'

'When? How?'

'I wanted to have your baby.'

Huge fissures were opening in this conversation.

'Have a baby? Back then? But you were only seventeen. You were a kid.'

'So what?'

Exactly. Yes. So what.

'You're being operatic,' he told her, 'you're the one who's into fantasy now – motherhood-romance shit.'

'Yes, maybe. But I still think it would have been the right thing to do. A "venturesome thing" to do.'

His word.

He was *taken aback*. That was the phrase. He couldn't find response for this revelation any more than he could for the first. He was getting no clean response back from his sensibility. He'd placed no importance at all on the long-forgotten conversation about having a baby. He was taken aback. He was at sea.

'Well, I hope you really are OK.' he heard himself say, 'and I hope we do meet up in the future. The near soon future. Anything you ever need – you just have to ask. You know that.'

Except, he expected her to say, for a baby.

She laughed, 'Your voice has changed again – you sound almost brotherly. But I must go now.'

Brotherly, he was not.

'Take care of yourself.'

'I do. I know how to – very well. Goodbye.'

He wanted to hold onto the call but he was conversationally *at sea*.

'Goodbye then.'

'Yes, goodbye. And you take care too.'

'Yes – but unlike you I don't think I know how to do that yet, properly.'

'Oh you take care of yourself quite well enough I seem to remember. And you're a big boy now – you are an older man. Now.'

The call ended. He was very much *at sea*.

Over a drink in the bar he argued with himself that he hadn't in any way 'inducted' her, although the idea of doing so had an erotic charge for him. Maybe it could be argued that it was inherent in the flow and nature of all contemporary male and female dynamics – something like that. Surely it was obvious that she had a predisposition. He certainly admitted to whore–fantasy shit. There was all that about his great-grandmother – herself, well, a whore. But that had been a game with Belle. But as he brooded, this was followed by stray concern about her health, her life moves. But most of all he was caught in the turbulence coming from the inadequacy of his personal code in response to what she had told him, the carnal discomfort and paradox that she was no longer available to him yet was available to random others. But the responses of his mind were not complete, late returns, he knew, would come.

Edith was obviously fidgeting with curiosity and from the queer possessiveness towards him which she had allowed to take shape in her mind. She did however wait as long as she could at breakfast before asking him how his telephone call had gone.

'Did you make contact then – with your own true love?'

'She is not my "true love",' he said, in a shielded voice, thinking that she could have so easily become his 'own true love' and maybe yet so become – she had always been so frighteningly full of potential for him.

'Well whatever,' Edith said.

'She's involved with a man in London. A Parisian.'

'It's honourable enough to lose out to a Parisian.' she said, with the pointless relief of her voice commingled with the pointlessness of her remark. 'It sounded very much like a middle-age crisis love affair to me.'

What the hell would she know about it?

'I don't see myself as "middle-aged" – I don't think that description has any meaning and certainly doesn't carry a fixed program of behaviour.'

'I didn't mean to offend.'

'I wanted to do a pilgrimage to the Spanish Civil War sites with her. And to visit anarchist places. I wanted to fit it in after we finish up here, we'd planned it for some time.'

She ate her cheese and cold cuts, wary of speaking.

He pushed his breakfast platter across to her. 'You have that. I'll just have coffee.'

'Thank you. But I couldn't eat it.'

She would.

She then said, 'I'd love to see Spain again. I was there many years ago, I hate to admit it – before, just before, the Civil War. Yes, I'd like to see Spain again. I knew Ascaso, one of the brilliant minds on the anarchist side. I knew him. . .well.'

This lured him out of his brooding, into bright surprise. He realised, of course, that it was feasible. But for him Edith had not had a personal history, let alone an existence before he was born. His knowledge of her had been from their day-to-day travelling, their IAEA itinerary. Back in Australia, he realised, he had seen her as a biographical note – 'leading environmentalist'.

Ascaso was a name from a poem for him, and from his reading in anarchist history.

'Did you know Durruti?'

'No. I would have liked to have, but no.'

She began to eat his breakfast, now aware that she had impressed him.

'I've abandoned the Spanish plans,' he said, realising that he had to say it to void her suggestion that maybe she should go with him. 'Anyhow it was sentimental anarchism, a hangover from another part of my life.' In a different tone so as to close the matter entirely, he said, 'I should try to sit in on the consultative committee to stop some of the silliness that will come out.'

She changed her tone too, 'You're hard on the others. Remember giving "public concern" a voice is part of our brief.'

They knew each other's views and relapsed into silence. He would talk to her at another time about Spain and the anarchists. He feared that now it would painfully enliven his numbed heart.

'If you change your mind about Spain – I would gladly come along to keep you company. But don't expect me to help with the driving. I dare say it's not that much different from back home but I do recall many donkeys and flocks of sheep.'

She was asking to go with him.

'No. Thank you Edith. I've given up on the Spanish adventure.'

'You poor boy, you make it sound so tragic.'

'No, I don't,' he said, irritated, glad to be irritated with her. 'It is not tragic at all. It's just something that's passed through my life. Abandoned plans. Acceptable losses. Nothing tragic.'

• DISPOSAL •

He explained to Edith that he wanted to work it so that he spoke last at the plenary session of one of the Commissions related to the IAEA.

'I don't want the Russian to speak last.'

Edith found the idea offended her sense of the natural order of things.

'You have to accept these things as they occur,' she said.

She moved the flowers on the breakfast table and straightened her setting, staring into the flowers as if she were looking into the foliage of her seventy years of life and now fearing that everything in her life might have been ordered, not by the natural scheme of things, but by 'schemers' like him.

Maybe *his* life, the moves and plays of his life, were being induced by others.

'I don't like schemers,' she said, 'and you have already involved me in some sort of trickery with that girl.'

He hunted his mind for a reason which might swing her.

'Let's do it for Australia,' he sang, 'let's do it because we're mates.'

'You don't mean that,' she said matter-of-factly, wishfully.

Although he and Edith were far apart in political sentiment and personality, and age, they had been oddly bonded. They did represent Australia in an official way and were travelling on official passports, married in a file by a public servant. She clung to him socially because she was not a good mixer. And she'd fallen into a dependency on him because he was on secondment, temporarily, to the IAEA, while she was a public member of the mission. This meant she 'left things to him' as a dependent wife might and this sponsored extraneous echoes of matrimony.

'I just don't like schemers,' she said, 'never have done.'

'Oh come on Edith – treat it as a game – a scam.'

'I can't really treat the problem of nuclear waste as some sort of *game*,' she said solemnly, 'I'm sorry.' And then she added, 'I don't know what a scam is.'

'Who got you a better room here at the hotel?' He reached across and placed his hand on hers, which surprised him and surprised her. She looked down at his hand – he hoped it didn't look as manipulative as it felt, under her glance.

He took his hand away.

'Who got you out of the meeting with the guy from the Netherlands whom you detest?'

The thirty years' difference in their ages made the touch an unnatural advance and recalled for him – and he guessed for her – the ambiguous visit to her room he'd made one drunken night. Oh God.

'I did chase that girl's telephone number all across the world for you, which, in all likelihood, you should not have had. No, I don't like schemers.'

The breakfast food disappeared as Edith wolfed it down. He gestured to the waiter and in his faltering German ordered another round of breakfast for her.

'You can't bribe me with food and you shouldn't encourage me to eat,' she said, as if to an over–indulgent lover. 'You know I eat too much.'

She liked to play, verbally, with this marrying.

'Maybe Dr Kum'a Ndumbe would do it,' he pondered aloud. The Cameroon Commissioner and he had something of a common view of things, got along well. He didn't quite know why.

This seemed to get at Edith, maybe she felt now excluded by this suggestion and would rather be implicated than excluded.

'What is your plan then,' she asked, in a right–to–know voice, 'hypothetically speaking?'

'It's simple,' he said, 'there are seven reports to be given – I'm in number five position. The Soviet guy Ulyanov has got last place – he demanded it for godsake at the Secretariat meeting. Well, I'm going to take it away from him – and that's where you come in.'

'If I do come in. If I choose to play politics.'

'All you have to do is deliver a message to the chairperson during the fourth report. This message will call me from the dais and while I'm gone Ulyanov will be forced to speak in position six. I'll come back and give my report in the last position. Get it?'

She stared at him as if suspecting that something remained unsaid. 'But really, why?'

'The last speaker gets the last say.'

'Why's that so important?'

'It just is. You get the last say.'

'It's a form of cheating.'

'Do you think they don't cheat? What about Ulyanov's famous news release on Wednesday? It's just gamesmanship, Edith.'

'Really you're just little boys.' Then her face indicated she would do it. 'You're corrupting me,' she said, with a coyness.

He thought she was tantalised by the intrigue as she had been when she'd found the girl's telephone number for him. He thought she even enjoyed the possibility of corruption at her age – as though it testified that she had life left to corrupt, innocence to lose.

'And we're assuming that I agree with the things you'll say when you get this much-treasured last position.'

He wasn't sure about giving her a veto.

'I think I should have the right to see what you intend to say – which I assume is not strictly FA policy,' she said.

'Even you, Edith, agree that being well-meaning isn't enough in negotiated positions.'

She looked confused and as if she might bolt.

'I just don't want Australia to come out of this as dupes in some ridiculous manifesto,' he said.

'All right then, as long as I get to read what you're going to say first.'

'Yes.'

He gave her hand a squeeze, spontaneously this time, 'Terrific – as co-conspirator, Edith, your timing will be everything.'

'Don't care for the expression "co-conspirator".'

'Adventuress then – you are a bit of an adventuress, Edith.'

She made a small pleased mouth. Under the earnest eminent

environmentalist there really was an adventuress. 'And remember,' she said, 'I'm just indulging you. I only hope that it's all harmless.'

On the night of the plenary he rehearsed her.

'I'll feel very silly,' she said, 'if I begin to giggle.'

He saw the seventy-year-old Edith on the platform with a piece of paper in her hand, giggling in front of the Commission people. He wondered about the image she had of herself – was it unsynchronised with her age? Could she still at times see herself as a giggling schoolgirl?

'You're a good actress, Edith, when you faked that call to Australia for the telephone number you were perfect.'

'Don't recall it – I still feel bad about all that.'

By talking about it that way he was *not* recalling it. By keeping it up in the conversational air like a kite he could avoid it. The telephone call had been an emotional devastation, objectively, although the expected emotional concussion had not arrived. What was disturbing him about it was that the concussion had not reached him, had not *authentically* reached him, that it was still out there waiting to hit him.

Or did he really like the idea that the seventeen–year-old schoolgirl he'd met and loved was now in London doing a little amateur whoring? No. Why did he say 'A little amateur whoring'? She'd said she was whoring. The girl was now a whore.

Well, I'm no longer your archetypal young girl. I'm no schoolgirl any longer. I'm grown up and worse. . .I'm older than I should be. . .

Have you been through some sort of tribulation?

You could say that.

Stop being mysterious.

As they say, a girl has to eat. . .you inducted me. . .you taught me how to pleasure older men. You let me down. I wanted to have your baby.

Rubbish.

He supposed he felt he should have an emotionally devastating concussion from all this and was more worried that he seemed deficient than he was worried about her. He'd reacted lubriciously to the conversation – that also worried him. Or he worried that he *should* be worried about it and wasn't. His personal code had no response ready for him. He was uncomfortably skewered by it but could not react. Skewered.

• • •

On the last night he sat through the political posturings of the other Commission members and despaired of diplomacy at this level. He either found this sort of international posturing 'subtly critical' for world affairs or 'frighteningly futile'. He was finding it, tonight, frighteningly futile.

He saw that, as planned, Edith was absent from the horseshoe of Commissioners and auditors as he sat apart with seven other rapporteurs. All those in the conference room wore headphones for simultaneous translation which gave them the appearance of each being lost in a private Walkman world.

It was approaching the time when Edith should appear and come forward with the note. Number four - Lenrie Peters of Gambia - was rising to speak.

He saw her appear fleetingly at the side door of the conference room, look around and disappear back into the anteroom. She then appeared again. He gave her a disguised nod. She shook her head and made a desperate movement of her mouth to say that she couldn't go through with it.

Damn her.

She was probably entranced by this demon dance around the issue of radioactive waste, fearful of disrupting the incantations.

He silently cursed her.

She must have sensed the fury of these curses because he saw her look at the floor for a second or two and then stride in and come in at the side of the rapporteurs.

She passed him without a glance and handed the faked note to the chairperson. She then turned in a calculated way, controlled in her pacing like a fashion model and, again without glancing at him, left the dais.

The chairperson read the name on the note and passed it along to him. He made as to read it - it said 'You and your boyish games!' - frowned histrionically, looked at his watch, took off his headphones, and leaned across to the chairperson. She took off her headphones.

'I'm needed off-stage for a moment - I'll be back as soon as I can,' he whispered urgently under the booming voice of the Gambian rapporteur.

The chairperson looked perplexed. 'But you are next to report,' she hissed.

'Go on without me - I'll be back as soon as I can - I'll be back before it's over. Go on with Ulyanov.'

'I don't like changing the order of things. . .' she looked at her watch as it if might give her advice.

'Don't worry - I'll be back.'

He left, chortling to himself, conscious of the questioning gaze of Ulyanov and the others.

He found Edith standing with a bored security officer chatting in limited English.

'Well done Edith - well done - did you receive my curses?'

'Yes, I did indeed, but I was rather good, I thought.'

'You were.'

From where they stood, Edith could see the dais and she reported that Ulyanov had risen to speak, disconcerted, unwilling.

They listened to him begin his report, waited a few minutes, and then he returned to the conference room.

When Ulyanov finished, the unsmiling chairperson beckoned him to make the final report.

Afterwards, at the drinks and the irradiated shrimp - sanitised by gamma rays - which Edith wouldn't touch, the chairperson came across to him and said, 'I cannot understand. Why should you be called from proceedings at such a time?'

Edith, who was standing near him nervously sipping her wine, turned away.

He shrugged and said, 'Affairs of state.'

'At such a time?' she persisted.

'My Minister called from Australia. But apart from that I thought it all went rather well, didn't you?' he said to the chairperson, turning briefly to take another canapé, winking at Edith.

He saw Ulyanov, the almost suave Russian, pushing his way through the crowd towards him. Ulyanov arrived with a quizzical-eyed smile, implying that he had an inkling of what had happened. Ulyanov swept him aside with his arm and at the same time stopped a drink waiter and took two drinks, handing one to him. 'Tell me Commissioner Australia - what went on there tonight eh!? I, Ulyanov, begin the evening as the concluding rapporteur, the finale, but now the evening is over and I find myself not having been finale: Australia is finale and your message of criticism of ordinary citizen peace workers becomes the finale. Ulyanov asks: how could that have come about when finale was the Soviet's negotiated and rightful place? How?'

'These things happen, Commissioner.'
'These things happen? These things must not happen!'
Ulyanov chuckled away the tone of his complaint.

Next day he had a call from Ulyanov suggesting they meet for
'something of a cultural exchange' at a non-official level. They had
finished the evening on joking terms and the invitation was not
unexpected.

Ulyanov suggested that they meet at the bar of the Sacher. 'But we
will not talk Synroc or borosilicate.'

He agreed but after putting down the telephone he had second
thoughts and worried about the protocol of such a meeting. He rang
the Political Officer just to have the meeting noted but the Political
Officer laughed and suggested that maybe Ulyanov wanted to defect.
'But more likely, just get drunk. Watch out you don't get caught with
the bill.'

'An expensive venue,' he said, greeting Ulyanov who was drinking
champagne, a bottle of champagne sitting on the bar in an ice bucket.

'Australia is a rich country, is it not?'

Did that mean that Australia was meant to be picking up the bill?

'So is Comecon.'

Ulyanov worked with Comecon.

Ulyanov pulled an ambiguous face. 'We are budget cutting. I
admire your clothes – beautiful cotton. I see you in a silk suit one
session – very nice.'

'Have you had me under observation?'

He wondered if Ulyanov were gay and if this was a pass.
Ulyanov poured him a glass of champagne.

'I have a passion for clothing,' Ulyanov laughed.

He glanced at Ulyanov's rather well-cut, tailor-made but obviously
Russian suit. His cufflinks were Air India and his tie clip from Olivetti.
Ulyanov's shoes were pointed, grey, in some sort of Italian youth-
style which was wrong for him.

'You don't do so badly yourself,' he said, dishonestly.

Ulyanov grimaced. 'In Russia we do not have variety,' but he
seemed pleased with the compliment, 'I do the best I can.'

'I have not forgiven you Australia, I suspect unfair play last night –
and you a sporting nation!'

'What about your news release which some of us on the sub-
committee didn't get to see!'

Ulyanov put an arm on his shoulder. 'Never mind all that. I have an affection for you Australia – I find something of myself in you. And I have a proposition for you also.'

He waited for the proposition. Maybe Ulyanov was going to try to recruit him.

Ulyanov drank from the champagne, preparing his words. 'Tell me – do you like caviare?'

'Yes, I've never really ever had enough.'

'That is as it should be, my friend – one should never satisfy oneself with caviare. But I'm about to offer you an opportunity to do so. I have three kilos of first class caviare – Beluga Prime – arrived yesterday from Soviet Union beautiful – an Aeroflot official has. . .well. . .presented it to me – in return for a service.'

Ulyanov looked pleased with himself, pleased that he showed perhaps a flair for Western–style wheeler-dealing. He sipped his champagne, closing his eyes to savour it without distraction. 'I want to offer you an opportunity to take a share of this caviare – it is in half–kilo cans – a nice gift. Or eat it in your hotel room. A feast. It's as you say, "top of market".'

Ulyanov delivered his offer in an imitation of Western 'salesmanship'.

'I will definitely say yes.'

'Good! Let us to negotiations.'

'I'll take perhaps two cans – if the price is right.'

'Boy have I got a deal for you.' Ulyanov said this with relish, relishing the phrase, again, for its Westernness.

He pulled up his heavily cufflinked shirt to expose a watch calculator. He took out a silver pencil – it looked like a public relations gift but the name of the company had worn away – and used the point to punch up his calculations.

'Do you think 500 DM is a fair price?' Ulyanov asked.

'I know that caviare was selling at US$15 at Christmas – it was in the *New Yorker*.'

'I read that,' Ulyanov said, 'so you see it is a bargain I offer you.'

'That was retail.'

He tried to make the US$–DM–A$ conversion in his head – and then the ounce–gram conversion.

'But if you pay in dollar-A,' Ulyanov said, 'we must consider that it is weakening against the basket of currencies.'

Ulyanov turned away from negotiations to ask the barman for a napkin, with which he dabbed his mouth.

'But we're not weakening against the rouble.'

'I work in dollars US.'

Ulyanov had all the conversions clear in his head of course, but switched about to muddy the calculations he was trying to make in his head and they concluded the deal without him having any feel for the reasonableness or otherwise of it. They then drank champagne and talked of great dinners they'd eaten.

After one of the pauses in the conversation, Ulyanov asked thoughtfully, 'Tell me Australia, if we were at war could you shoot me?'

'Yes.'

Ulyanov nodded, pondered.

'But here at the Commission I listen to you – you are a man without passion. You are the man who raises clever doubts. How could you act?'

'The important thing is to be able to act decisively while in doubt.'

Again they stood in silence with their champagne, while Ulyanov pondered this, then put a hand on his shoulder and said, 'But now we are living – not shooting. Why don't we leave now and I will take you to a House of Pleasure. On the Gurtel. They will be good to us.'

It was at this moment that he felt that the delayed response to the telephone call to his girlfriend should begin, the concussion hit.

But it did not.

What fell on him was the bill for two bottles of Moët et Chandon. Ulyanov had only roubles, had 'overlooked' changing some money that day.

Thoughts came to him as he paid the bill, of a similar invitation made a few years earlier by a Nigerian at a conference, the brothel bonding, or in the mind of the Nigerian some sort of male combativeness, although he had not fully comprehended the nature of the Nigerian's challenge.

He saw crudely again that while she, the girl, was denied to him she was available to all others, say to Ulyanov. But again he registered this without reaction. No emotional lightning struck his heart.

'Zweig, Stefan Zweig – you know of this writer?' Ulyanov asked as they left.

'Yes, vaguely, he's on the Vienna reading list.'

'Well Zweig, he went to this House.'

'Is there a plaque?'

'Plaque? Plague? Is there disease?'

'No – is there an historical marker – a sign saying Zweig went to this place?'

Ulyanov laughed, realising that he had misunderstood the language and then he made it a joke, 'There is no plaque in Vienna. A joke, Australia, a joke.'

He roared with laughter as they went out into the night.

• A PORTRAIT OF A WHORE •

He rang her again when he got to London, despite his earlier rebuff, and this time, after some further resistance, she agreed to meet him for a drink.

They met in the lounge of the Basil where he 'stayed when in London'.

'I've always wanted to be able to say the phrase "where I stay when I'm in London",' he said nervously.

'Yes, you would. I work in Knightsbridge,' she said, neutrally, 'so it's all very convenient. And I've done a few out-calls in the Basil.'

'Oh, so you know it.' His voice was not as neutral as he would have liked.

She had the jauntiness at twenty-two both of the schoolgirl he'd known and also of a girl who was at home on a bar stool. Being at home on a bar stool together with a use of cosmetics to give emphasis to her youth, both things rippled through her style.

She wore a full-length light white linen coat.

She opened the coat to show a pink silk dress presenting her cleavage and her body line, holding out a leg to display her stockings, her patent high–heeled shoes. 'Well, how do I look?' She smiled teasingly at him, 'Don't tell me - I know how I look.'

'You look delicious,' he said, 'you haven't changed. . .' That was not quite right and not quite the right thing to say. 'Age has not wearied you nor the years condemned. . .' Not much better.

'You really mean that you thought that it would make me into some decrepit hag, that sin would have scored my features.' She laughed, drinking down her vodka and tonic and deepening her voice for effect, but said, 'I look like a whore: I mean to look like a whore.'

'Well, you said when I called from Vienna that you'd "changed". I did expect the worst.' That was also weakly diplomatic.

'Not really,' she said, pensively, 'not at all, really.' adding with a childlike smile, 'I hope.'

She was no longer his schoolgirl lover or the university student and although he'd tried to prepare himself for this, he had not succeeded. He wasn't sure whether she was now his peer, and her adultness, her glamour, the female strength of her 'role' all bothered him, almost unmanned him. When he'd suggested they drink a martini for old times' sake she'd declined saying, 'God, who drinks martinis these days - you are really the last Scott Fitzgerald of the world.' If only he were.

She'd been slow to show interest in his work with the IAEA and the other things he'd done in the last few years. She laughed again and said, 'My God, and you were the one who used to say that the bomb had already dropped - inside us,' and again adopting a deep, stagey voice, ' "we are the dead in our own life-time".'

'That was my period of nihilistic posturing,' he said, laughing along with her, falsely. 'I don't say that now. I'm really only interested in it as a technical and negotiating problem. Australia's very good on the problem of inspections. I don't think of it as a street issue any more.' God that sounded dull.

'Now, what else did you say in those days?' she said, making an effort of recollection. 'What about always defending the smaller polity against the larger polity. Do we still say that?'

He considered that she might have passed him in worldliness and intellectually, he found himself bemused by her use of words such as polity while she sat swinging on a bar stool, dressed as a whore in silk.

'I have added a refinement to that position,' he said, foggily. 'I'm interested in the way we are governed by forums other than recognisable political forums. We are governed by the dead. Maybe the dead are the strongest polity. I've moved economics down the list.

I enjoy the elegant paradox of nuclear deterrence. Or the inelegant paradox.'

'Do you now,' she said, lightly mocking.

'I guess you're not interested in all that.'

'Why? Because I do some whoring? You think I've given up on political science? Do you see it as a switch from mind to cunt? Do you think I'm incapable of using both at once?' She laughed at him.

He blushed.

'I feel out of my depth,' he made a gesture of helplessness, waved a hand at her demeanour.

'Come on now. I'm just kidding you along.' She touched him, the first touching of their meeting, except for a sisterly kiss when they met. 'Come on, be the sophisticate, I always look to you as the sophisticate. You were the first man I met who tipped.'

An impossible command. In his mind he gathered together his scrapbook of credentials, scrappy evidence of his 'sophistication'. He'd talked with Carter, Brezhnev. He'd published important papers. He'd stayed in the finest hotels in the greatest of cities. He'd been drunk with ambassadors, heads of state. He'd been a part of historic occasions. But he had not become a writer. He had not become a Scott Fitzgerald. He had not become a great chemist either.

'Do you still want to fuck me?' she asked, returning her lips to the straw in her drink.

He had tried during the meeting so far to push this physical desire for her away, to safeguard himself against desiring the unobtainable, accepting also that her initial resistance to seeing him signalled a contracted involvement with her 'boyfriend'. But he now sensed that she needed to know whether he still desired her, that she was wanting something from him now, confirmation maybe that she retained some sexual status in the normal world, or at least, the world he came from.

He tried to sound casual, his desire heated to lubricity, 'I thought we had put all that aside.'

She sat formulating a response, no ready response having glided from her bright lips.

'I thought we had too,' she said, 'but we haven't.' Her voice suggested that this was not for her an entirely happy realisation.

'Your voice has changed again,' she said, but this time kindly. 'Come on then, let's finish these drinks and go up to your room.' She paused, looked across the top of her glass, 'Or would you like to come to my apartment? More precisely, the apartment I work from?'

He took a drink, he was now swamped by lubricity, her glow of adolescence was mingled with fantasies of whoredom, together with, all together with, their own erotic history. It was a dreadfully powerful surge of desire and so great was his fear of still being denied it at the last instant that he wished profoundly that they had finished, done it, that it was all over or that all desire was absent. He found he almost wished for a return to the low libido which he'd had during a hepatitis attack.

'Well,' she asked, in a voice which suggested she knew the answer, 'which is it to be?'

He began to answer untruly, to say he'd prefer his room, so as not to reveal how victimised he was by fantasies of whoredom, when she interrupted, 'I should tell you,' she said, again as if she knew its effect, 'that I've just come off work – that's why I'm dressed like a tart.'

'It doesn't worry me in the least.'

She laughed. 'When you rang me from Vienna your voice went like that.'

'I'm nervous for godsake. It's been some time, a few hundred years since we went to bed.'

'Maybe you're not sure?'

'I desire you very much.'

'Good. I desire you.'

They took each other's hand.

'Let's go to your place, I want to see it, as part of you.' He tried to control the tone of his lie, but gave up and decided to go to the truth, 'No I want to go to it because it would be an incredible turn–on.'

She laughed with relief at their having reached some sort of simple candour.

The place was upstairs, through a doubly locked door – a flatette – freshly painted – well–tiled bathroom, piles of towels, a large satin–covered bed, low lights, prints or photographs of David Hamilton–style girls.

'Tasteful – in a whorish kind of way,' he said, enjoying the relief of being able to say the word.

'It is meant to be "tasteful in a whorish kind of way",' she said. 'We run a class act here,' she said in her mock, street–tough voice, 'we even advertise in the *Herald Tribune*.'

He took her fur coat and she came into his arms.

'Let's go to bed,' she whispered. She went from him to the bathroom, calling to him 'put your clothes on the chair, love, there's a hanger for your coat.' She poked her head out from the bathroom, 'Sorry, force of habit, it just came out.'

She went on with her bathroom activity, but called again, 'Oh, another thing – sorry about this – but could you put £100 in the jar in case Johnny comes and finds us. . .'

'Johnny?'

'The Man. The guy who runs this place.'

'Oh.' He guessed he understood. He took the money from his wallet and put it in the jar on the mantelpiece.

She came from the bathroom. 'There really should be another girl working tonight but she's sick. We'll get the money back as we're leaving – it's just a precaution against misunderstanding. Johnny's not a man you want any misunderstanding with.'

When he turned from putting the money in the jar she was lying naked on the bed.

'Do I look different?' she asked.

He gazed at her beautiful body. 'Beautiful, beautiful.'

'What about my breasts?'

'Beautiful.'

'Aren't they more attractive?'

'They were always attractive.'

He joined her on the bed.

'They are larger,' she said, fondling her breasts. 'The bastards talked me into it. Some days I'm horrified but generally I suppose I prefer it. They wanted me bigger. There's this other girl,' she assumed her tough voice, 'Sex Queen of the West End. Well, Johnny wanted me to be bigger than she and they talked me into having them enlarged. Voilà!'

'Like Mariel Hemingway,' he said, feeling that he was politely trying to normalise her behaviour.

'Yes. Like Mariel Hemingway. Obviously you're not turned off by it.'

'No.'

She laughed. 'But they still have me on an anorexic diet. Children's portions. The Brits like the idea of a woman's breasts on a girl's body. And the Arabs. And probably every man in the whole fucking world.'

As they began to make love he felt compelled, against his civilised self, to ask her how often she'd been in the bed that day.

'There's that funny voice again,' she said playfully, 'four or five and you make six.'

'And your boyfriend, I suppose, this morning.'

'Oh yes him. He's into all this whore-fantasy shit too.' She laughed. 'But of course with him it's no fantasy.'

He dissolved into the eroticism she spun and she ceased to be either the archetypal seventeen–year–old or the New Sex Queen of the West End and instead became a complete and overwhelming other presence.

As they were leaving she said, 'I said a lie before.'

'Yes.'

'Back at the Basil I said I dressed like this for work. Well. . .' she gave a grim smile as she secured all the locks, 'I sort of always dress like this. It makes me feel less split. When I wasn't working I used to dress like Princess Di, an English girl out of *Country Life*, and one day I said, hell, I'm a whore, I'd rather be dressed like one. Well maybe not always like a whore. But I guess my style is "expensive sexy" now. It feels right.'

'I'm frightened by how much I like it. We're still good in bed together.'

'Yes, we are.'

Out in the street she said, 'Well, this is where we have to say goodbye.'

'No chance of dinner?'

'No.'

'Look, if you need help – or your fare back to Australia. . .'

'You're generous to offer. But I'm well off. I don't need money but I'll keep your offer in mind. I'll go on doing what I'm doing for now.' She put on her gruff voice. 'Puts me in touch with myself.'

'OK.'

'It's good for my feminist critique. I'm learning from being a spectacle.'

'I don't really understand.'

'I'll explain it one day.'

'I'll take you up on that.'

'What will you do in London? You said, I remember, something about taking me to Hazlitt's grave or old rooms. But I don't think I can really go sightseeing with you. I'm on a tight rein, one way or another.' She took his arm. 'What about you? You seem to be living near the edge despite your international diplomacy and all that.'

'Oh yes, I feel close to the edge sometimes but I have a job to do.'

'I remember! Another thing you used to say – you used to say, "It's no use asking me about nuclear disarmament because I have a death wish".'

He smiled as he heard his words.

'Do you still have?'

'I'm still alive. But I say now that all international negotiation for disarmament has to be based on total distrust. The IAEA is a body founded on distrust. That's why I like it. It tries to take trusting people out of negotiations by developing techniques for verification and inspection. I believe in negotiated distrust.'

He added, 'That's probably why I ended up there. I put my faith in distrust now.'

For the first time she seemed to like something he'd said.

He was already seeing tomorrow's looming desire for her and facing now again the possibility of denial.

He said, concealing this from his voice, 'You'll see me tomorrow?'

'Professionally?' she said, leaning into him. 'No, of course I'll come to the Basil at three. We'll do something. But I must rush now.' She gave a wry smile, wrapped her coat tightly about herself and moved off refusing the admiring glances from passing males.

She turned and made a kiss. 'It's a weird world I'm in now.'

As he walked away from her he remembered that she hadn't retrieved the £100 from the jar in her apartment. She would bring it tomorrow, he guessed.

He wondered if he would introduce her to Edith his unwanted travelling companion, who had foisted herself on him following the completion of their official business in Vienna.

'We'll go our own ways.' she'd said when they'd been in Vienna, 'but it seems silly for us to split up if we're both going to be in London and then going on business together in Israel.'

Edith called the next morning, on the telephone from her room at the Basil, to see what he was doing that day.

'How did your reunion go with your lost love?' she asked, trying to exclude from her voice any suggestion that she vied with the younger woman for his time, or that she, Edith, had any claim on him – yet these ridiculous and unreasonable shadows were there.

'She is not, as you know, my "lost love", Edith, although I wish she were in some ways my found love and yes, I've lost her. It is all in the past.'

That didn't sound very coherent.

'You are fortunate that you have so little in your past,' she said. 'I trust, anyhow, you had a pleasant enough evening.'

'Yes.'

He'd become quite drunk on his own in his room watching television and had then for a time sat in silence.

'I didn't,' she said, accusingly, 'I ate at the place around the corner and found it execrable – you were going to recommend a place but of course with your urgent personal life you went off without a word. I'm afraid the places I used to know around here have long gone.'

He let the complaint pass.

'Anyhow I thought,' she continued, 'that you might like to make it up to me by coming to the Summer Exhibition at the British Academy – we could walk from here. Do us good.'

'I'm seeing my friend, I'm afraid, Edith.'

'Oh? Again? Things must not have gone so badly then. You should watch that you don't allow yourself to be hurt again.'

This was a new kind of advice. This was not matrimonial, this was, this was maternal. That was too much.

'Oh go to hell Edith – I'm afraid I can't squire you around London. I'm sorry, but no. That's not my role.'

'You mean you can't waste your time squiring around an old woman.'

'I found your advice a trifle maternal.'

'I don't know which is the more insulting,' there was a pause, 'I thought you were more sophisticated – I thought of you as a friend.'

She was lying to herself. Ah for the pure *friend*.

'I'm afraid, Edith, that I do have my own business to do here.'

'You didn't seem to object that much in Vienna. I can remember times when you were the one glad of company, glad of a friendly face at breakfast. And, I dare say, you will feel the same way when we resume our business in Israel.'

'This is London. This is a personal visit. We are not required to be together.'

'I well appreciate that,' she said, coldly, 'all I was asking of you was whether you would. . .' she now enunciated each word, 'accompany/ me/to/the/Royal/Academy.'

'No. I will not. I have, repeat, my/own/things/to/do/if/you/don't/ mind.'

He hung up on her.

Oh God, that had all sounded sickeningly matrimonial. He had no sense of being severed from her at all, he'd gained nothing from having spoken his feelings. The exchange would heighten his awareness of Edith for the rest of the day in a perturbing way. And, simultaneously, he was in a welter of desire for the girl, and an agony of fear that he would be denied her by something. 'Girl whore.' he said it aloud to himself, 'girl whore.'

Then he said, 'Old bitch, old bitch.'

I'm going crazy.

He began to dress. Would he change his clothes before meeting her? How should he fill the time before she came? I'm going crazy.

He left the Basil intending to go to a gallery to fill time. The Royal Academy Summer Exhibition was usually a mess. He could walk a little further to the National.

He had to walk by the Royal Academy and as he did he felt he might as well look in. He tried to dismiss the chance of meeting Edith. 'I can go to the Royal Academy alone. I am in no way excluded simply because it was her wish that we go there together.'

He entered the gallery. He saw Edith at the other end of the gallery. He gave a nervous, jerky wave. She did not wave back but returned to her catalogue.

They moved about the gallery as if fixed on opposite ends of a long rod. He determined that he would not leave 'because of her'. He did not want his behaviour to be in any way determined by her existence. But he acknowledged that his consciousness of her was inescapable. The irritating thing was that he should be stuck like this, manoeuvring around a seventy-year-old woman in an art gallery, simply because a bureaucrat had placed their names, two strangers, together on a list of suggested delegates on a government mission.

He completed the rounds of the paintings, only half-seeing, aware that sometimes he and Edith drifted closer together but then a navigational correction would be made by either or both and they would move apart.

He lunched alone at Bentley's, which was far enough away from the Academy to avoid any coincidental meeting with Edith, and then returned to his room.

As he dressed to meet the girl he noted that in the past when visiting a brothel he had always shaved and considered his dress and personal hygiene, not wanting to show disrespect. It was after all some sort of a date, a special sort of personal transaction.

He thought he sometimes got the performance of 'going to a whore' right. When his mood and inclination was for nothing else   – when it was not a substitution for anything else or a pretence for something else. He sometimes desired the anonymous, unthreatening – or 'threatening' in its own peculiar way   –   autonomous sexual act which contained within it the very faint mimicry of love but was not intended as a substitute for it. It was still two humans exchanging something, a small conversation, a small physical act, a simple, limited, stylised touching of two human beings. Sometimes it worked so well, the prostitute acting and interacting slightly, and he the client, acting the client and also, sometimes, interacting in that slight, very slight way. It was such a perfectly 'simple' act but highly refined by history. It surprised him how often it contained simple 'good will'.

But this was more now, he was courting her, wanting maybe to win her back from her boyfriend. About 'Johnny' he was uncertain; he did not know how to approach the claims that Johnny might have on her. Maybe he really wanted to displace Johnny and to be both her lover and her pimp. How to dress as a lover? How to dress as a pimp? How to dress as a client ? Did pimps really have a style? How did that idea arise?

He went to the bar to wait and rehearse his conversation. He felt randy. A stirring of life.

Life, like a martini, should be stirred, not shaken. He'd say that to her.

He waited until she was well over three–quarters of an hour late. He then went to reception and asked if there was a message for him. Maybe she was 'working back'. There was a message. He opened it and it said that she had on second thoughts considered it best not to meet him again. 'Let's part while we're ahead.' She said she felt a special kind of love for him but nothing could be done about it just now.

Just now.

He felt a shock of thwarted desire. It was not that torment which came from withheld love, it was thwarted desire. No remedy presented itself. He did not want a drink. He wanted to court her but that really hadn't started. He was not lovesick, he was thwarted.

He went to his room, pulled off his so–carefully–tied bow tie, restless with lost equilibrium. He was annoyed that he felt, too, a slight cowardly marginal relief from not having to face her and the strangeness which surrounded her.

He tried laughing at his expectations. He saw himself swirling in fantasies from times past, a Berlin Weimar fantasy of decadence which he'd never found.

The telephone rang and he picked it up, relieved instantly from his turbulent condition, back on full longing alert for her, but it was not her, it was Edith.

'I rang to apologise,' she said, 'about my uncivil behaviour in the gallery this morning – I realised later that you'd come to, well, make a gesture, and I rebuffed you. I'm sorry. I was imposing on you. For that, also, my apologies. But thank you for coming to the gallery.'

'Oh,' he stumbled, 'oh that's all right, I was the one who was rude. I owe you an apology.'

'Well, I'm out of your hair. I'm booking into another hotel. I'll fade into the night. After all, we still have Israel to do. We'll see enough of each other.'

'That's not necessary, Edith. No. Don't go to that trouble.'

She was silent, wanting maybe further encouragement to stay.

He said, 'Let's have a drink.'

'A drink? It's a little early for me. But well, what the hell, yes.'

'I'll see you in the bar.'

'Will I get to meet your lady friend?'

'Oh no – I've put that off. How about we have a drink and then go down to Hazlitt's tombstone. In St Anne's.'

'Love to.' He felt her consciously not pressing for details of his personal life.

As he waited in the bar he read from Hazlitt: 'To live to oneself – what I mean by living to oneself is living the world as in it not of it: it is as if no one knew there was such a person and you wished no one to know that.'

• MARTINI •

He mixed the martini in the jug, stirring with studied performance. 'Always stirred never shaken,' he told her.

'I've never drunk a martini in my life.' She made it sound as if she were now fifty and had astoundingly missed the martini. Instead, she was seventeen and with no reason to have tasted a martini. 'We can pretend we are in New York.'

'Paris. It was actually invented by a Frenchman.'

'All right. If you like you can be in Paris and I'll be in New York. I really want to be in New York.'

'That'd be no fun.'

'We could call each other from those night–club table telephones.'

'I like to know the vermouth is there.' he said, scholastically, sniffing the jug for the vermouth, 'many don't. The great martini drinkers just want the gin mixed with mystique. Let the beam of light pass through the vermouth bottle and strike the gin – that was sufficient, sayeth Luis Buñuel.'

'Who is Luis Buñuel again? I know you told me once.'

'Buñuel is a Spanish film director. When we are in Spain we'll go. . .'

'. . .*Belle de Jour*! Right?'

'Correct. I took you to see it in some town in Victoria.'

'What I remember is you at the motel afterwards.' She giggled.

'When we go to Spain we'll go to Buñuel's birthplace.'

'You made me take money from you.'

'Aragon.'

'You showed me how a whore does it. And why do we have to go to people's birthplaces?'

He hadn't answered that question before. 'You're too questioning. You go to see where the magic started. You go to see if you can be touched by the magic. To see if there is any left.'

He carefully carried the brimful martinis to her on the balcony of the beach house.

'You're incredible,' she said, taking her martini, 'you've even brought along the proper glasses. I know they're martini glasses, that much I do know.'

'The glass is half the drink.'

'As you always say.'

Was he beginning to repeat himself?

He looked out at the sea in which he'd swum as a boy. 'I've never made love to anyone here in my home town – you are the first. That's unbelievable in a way, given that I lived here until I was seventeen, your age. . .'

'I'm eighteen now – you keep forgetting.'

'Sorry. But it took me to this age, well, getting towards forty, to have sex in the place where I was born. Says something.' He tried to muse on this but nothing occurred to him.

'What does it say?'

'I don't know yet.'

'Was it different?'

He kissed her fingers, one still slightly pen-calloused from her schooling. 'It's always different with you.'

'No slimy answers,' she said, 'tell me how it was different. I want to know.'

'Did the earth move?'

'Don't make fun of me. Tell me.'

'Different because of "formative circuits",' he teased. 'Do you want me to say things like that?'

'Whatever screwing circuits. Tell me!'

'I think you seek poetry.' He couldn't tell her now. 'I'll tell you when I've worked it out. I'll write a sonnet.'

It was different because he was getting emotional cross-tunings. He was making the cross-tunings.

'Another thing,' he said, 'is that it's my parents' home. Or at least their beach house. Which will do.'

'Will do what?'

She bridled when she sensed he was using the conversation to talk to himself.

'Well there is always, you know, the mother, always the mother, if it's not the bed where I was conceived, it's near enough.'

'Yuck,' she moved swiftly away from that. 'It's a beautiful drink. I could become really hooked on martinis. But what do you do with the olive, do you eat it at the beginning or the end of the drink or is it just a. . .garnish or what?'

Garnish, nice word.

'That's a personal preference. It's useful to play with during conversation. You can prick it with the toothpick and the olive oil seeps out.' He did it. 'See, the olive oil comes into the drink.'

'The olive on the toothpick gives the drink an axis.'

Yes, she was right.

She pricked her olive.

But regardless of the cross-tunings he was getting, seeking, he wanted also to imprint at the very same time a uniqueness onto their experience. To mark her off from his crowded personal history. He had used up so much   –   she couldn't be his first, well, first anything just about, not first love, first wife, nor first adultery, not even his first seventeen-year-old   –   and he couldn't give her any of the body's six or seven significant virginities, although at seventeen   –   eighteen   –   she seemed also to have exhausted most of these herself. Well, not all. And some she had given him. And they did share one or two sensual firsts of the minor scale. He supposed he was trying to consecrate their experience by bringing her to his home territory, the aura of kin if not kin. Into the family beach home   –   almost home   –   if not as a bride then as someone in her own significant category. He wanted to rank her equal with love if not *as love*. He couldn't tell her this yet.

'The olive is like leaking radioactivity,' she said. She was preoccupied with nuclear war but not as an issue   –   more as a macabre firework or as a sort of video game.

'I'll give you a twist of lemon next,' he said, 'that's the other classic garnish.'

She moved against him, began to arouse him, but he was in another mood, and said, 'I thought this was the cocktail hour.'

'I want to get rid of that sad look you have.'

'I'm not sad.'

But cross-tunings were coming in across the sea from his youthful marriage to a girl from his home town (although they'd never had sex in their home town – except for some vaguely recalled, fumbled caressing on a river rock in bushland, a 'fully dressed rehearsal', which he chose not to count). And a crude, bizarre ejaculation in a classroom late one afternoon – but no entry. The cross-tunings were entries of ill-handled love, their artless fumbled living. . .

In the sedate lounge of the Windsor he called the waiter. 'This martini is too warm, we asked for it very cold and very dry. It is neither.'

He was relieved that at twenty he had got the complaint out, slowly, and with some force.

'Yes sir.' The waiter went to take their drinks away.

'Leave mine,' Robyn said. 'Mine's all right.' She put her hand out over the drink.

'Yes madam.' The waiter took only his drink. 'I'll bring a fresh martini, sir.'

The waiter moved away.

'You are a pain in the arse sometimes,' his wife said.

'I thought you were big on consumer rights. Waiter!'

The waiter turned and came back to the table. 'Take my wife's martini also – we'll both have a fresh one.'

'Yes sir.'

She let the waiter take the drink this time.

'You give me the shits,' she said.

'So much for our second anniversary.'

'Fighting with waiters isn't my idea of a good time. It's alcohol, isn't it? I thought that was all you cared about.'

He knew he'd complained as a way of getting at her. He didn't really care about the martini.

He wanted to be in New York drinking martinis in Costello's bar with Thurber. With the sophisticated Louise.

'I wish I was in New York. In Costello's, only the Americans know how to mix a martini.'

'What would you know about Costello's or New York?'

'Travel isn't the only way of knowing.'

'The martini was invented by a Frenchman, anyhow.'

'Crap.'

'Have it your own way, I read it in *Origin of Everything*.'

'Crap.'

'And stop big-noting yourself,' she went on, 'you're just a country boy – you've drunk only one martini before in your whole life. You get it all from Scott Fitzgerald and you get it wrong.'

He remained silent, stung, taking balm from a private relishing of a secret score against her – that on the day before they'd left on their anniversary trip to Melbourne he'd drunk martinis in bed with Louise.

He reached across to take her hand, reversing the mood to place her at a disadvantage, gaining himself virtue for making the move to heal the mood while at the same time continuing to relish Louise.

'I'm sorry,' she said, taking the blame onto herself.

'We don't have to stay the country boy and girl all our lives.'

'I'm quite happy to be the country girl,' she said, quietly. . .

'Stirred never shaken,' Louise said, putting a finger on his nose to emphasise her point, stopping him with her other hand.

He'd been doing an American bartender act with the cocktail shaker, Louise being the first person he'd known to own a cocktail shaker.

'That's how I've seen it done in American movies.'

Louise laughed. 'You have been going to the wrong movies. There are some cocktails we do that way, my love, but not the martini, never the martini.'

'That's how we do them in my home town,' he said, trying to joke over his naivety.

'I'd believe that.'

He put the shaker down and removed the top and looked into it, 'They seem all right, they haven't exploded.'

'They'll be bruised,' she laughed, 'or at least that's what an aficionado would say.'

'Should I throw them away and start again?'

'No – I'm sure we can drink them with impunity – and I have an idea.'

He stopped himself asking who the aficionados were.

He began to pour them but Louise again stopped him. 'Tch, tch,' taking away the wine glasses he'd taken out and bringing back martini glasses, 'a classic drink demands a classic glass. And my idea is that we take the martinis to the bedroom and watch the sun set over the city.'

She led him to her bedroom, he slightly trembling with desire, the martini slightly spilling.

Looking out on the city at dusk from her bed he felt regret that he should need to be doing this against his young wife, felt the abrasion of his spirit. But it was numbed away with the lust for Louise, Louise who had the skills of living and such completeness.

'What's wrong, love - guilt?' Louise asked.

'No,' he lied. . .

'What's the matter?' he turned over in bed to face the question from his seventeen-year-old - eighteen-year-old - girlfriend.

'Memories spooking about,' he said.

'But you said you hadn't brought anyone else here.'

'That's true,' he said, putting a hand to her face, 'but the heart is a hotel.'

He reached over and took his martini from beside the bed and finished it.

Where had his young wife learned about the origins of the martini back then? He had looked in the book *The Origins of Everything*, she hadn't got it from there.

'I don't want you thinking of other women while you are sexing on with me.'

He smiled. 'They have their rights.'

She rolled on to him and began to arouse him again.

'Mix another drink,' he said 'first.'

She left the bed and went into the bar, her naked, youthful grace tightened his heart. She looked into the cocktail jug.

'There's some left,' she said.

'It'll be mainly melted ice.'

He was taking from her the flavours of young, first love. She was trying out her own explorations.

'I'll make a new lot, tell me how,' she called.

He was collecting pleasures not taken when he'd been seventeen. He was taking also perhaps the last taste of pure youth.

The first martini, though, had honoured his ex-wife and Louise. This next one would be theirs.

'One part vermouth, five parts gin,' he called back to her, 'some would argue - but that's my mix now.'

```
┌─────────────────────────────────────────┐
│          • A PORTRAIT OF A •             │
│             VIRGIN GIRL                  │
│            (CIRCA 1955)                  │
│                                          │
└─────────────────────────────────────────┘
```

FROM JANUARY/
It's hard for me to say dearest. . .
It's hard for me to say 'dearest' for I've never written a letter headed
'dearest'. I know you start your letters that way but I'm sure you'll
understand that I mean it even if I can't write it. I'll learn because my
liking for you has increased greatly since June 12 last year and the
experience in Room 17 about which I cannot write (or think). I'm not
making a very good job of explaining myself, it's just that I've never
written real words of love before and I guess the first time is always
the hardest. The town hasn't changed one single bit except that it's
deader (after one month of you being in the city). It really died a long
time ago but it must be a good town. Why? Because you always say
'Only the good die young'. PS. The next letter will be from the Red
Cross Camp. I'm still your same old Robyn.

The flag ceremony was deeply moving. . .
The flag ceremony was deeply moving, with all delegates from
overseas lined up with flags and as each country was called the

                            120

delegates took their flag forward and pledged it to world peace. It gave me the best feeling of my life. I've talked to one person of a different colour for the first time in my life. His name is Carlos and he's from the Philippines. But the Americans are the camp favourites although Nancy and I outwit them in conversation and we've seen all the films they've seen. I'm having an American girl Jo-Anne to stay with me after the camp and brother I just dig her the most. I'm in a discussion group on how we can learn more about world affairs and so advance world peace. I suggested a world newspaper run by journalists from every country and published in every capital. Have to rush, Jo-Anne just called 'Get up you all'.

Back home again and everything is as dead as ever...
Back home again and everything is as dead as ever. I've realised though that a year's separation will be good for us and will prove to everyone how serious we are. But I'll only have school to write about and you'll have the exciting life of a newspaper office which isn't really fair. I met the new headmaster today, he's a Master of Arts and everyone said he's very brainy. He told me he wants to bring 'tone' to the school. I agreed. I really want to be in Sydney with you instead of stuck here with a lot of kids with minds around the age fourteen. My mind seems to have shot ahead to age seventeen (comes from mixing with a seventeen-year-old cadet journalist, I suppose).

FROM FEBRUARY/
You'll never be able to convert people...
You'll never be able to convert people to Steinbeck's style of realism or make them realise that only those without an open mind pick out the parts which are not so gentle, because we have a perfect example here at school. Eddie Lyons got *East of Eden* at Prize Giving Day remember and over the holidays he let Jennie read it and she told him it was filth, although she read it all the way through. She made Eddie read it although Eddie is not what you would call a big reader.

Friedman and I will have to work on them both this year but I don't hold out much hope that they'll join the Free Thinkers. The Head wears academic robes at school assembly to give the place a bit of tone. Fat chance.

Dearest, there I've used the word. . .

Dearest, there I've used the word and I hope it makes you happier. But I'm using it because it seems natural now and it didn't before. But the letters are hard for me to write because all the emotion inside me just doesn't get out onto the page. Your story about a strange jelly fish on page nine was great. What does it feel like to have your first story in print? Dad's now in favour of me becoming a shorthand typist. Because no one in our family has ever done the Leaving Certificate he sometimes thinks I should be a doctor and next week remembers that I'm a girl and thinks of shorthand and typing. Your letters are on the lounge room table when I get home from school and I then journey into my bedroom where I emotionalise. Penny's just put on *Sixteen Tons* which she does every morning and afternoon. Please tell me if you're sick of hearing about school but you do understand don't you. It's the thing I am at the moment.

At the local show I had a passion. . .

At the local show I had a passion to go to the shooting gallery but it took all my energy to lift the adjectival gun let alone shoot it. I watched a cow cocky and copied him. I shot a duck. Do you believe in hypnosis? I didn't at first but Azarah the Floating Lady had a hypnotist who put a spell on Freddie Hawker. Anyone who can get Freddie Hawker to eat soap must be for real. Although the idea of having a spell or trance put on me is frightening another part of me would like it very much methinks. Do you really take the communist side now? I'm having an awful time trying to keep awake after nine at night. You wouldn't have any of those 'pep pills' you talked about taking? Where did you get them and are they dangerous? I really don't know what's wrong with me. I sleep all Sunday. Dad says I need a tonic. Just kidding about those pills. Jill is not doing the Leaving Certificate this year because her boyfriend failed it last year and she didn't want to be better than him. Crazy. How can you drink whisky? Dad says it will burn your insides out. Please don't. Curious that you say you like the plastic raincoat smell. I think the smell is awful but everyone is wearing them now. Anyhow, how come you were close enough to this girl to know whether she smelled plastic-raincoaty? Here's a joke: An epistle is an apostle's wife. Why do you say that only Americans rhyme 'liquor' with 'slicker'?

• • •

The matter of religion worries me a lot. . .

The matter of religion worries me a lot because I don't believe it at all but the scripture lessons the minister gives make it sound so unquestionable. Only later talking to Friedman do I realise that it doesn't make sense. Rev. Benson asked me why I wasn't going to be confirmed. I had to tell him I didn't believe in it (which took some doing) and that my mother thought it was all popery. So he suggested afternoon tea with his wife and himself to talk. Me against them at afternoon tea. Help! You'll have to come to my rescue with a good book. How many times do I want to say love things to you but my feelings won't come out in words. I still can't seem to keep awake. I'm going to get something from the chemist. The strangest thing has happened. The Leader of our State Red Cross group is coming to call on me – remember I met him at the camp at Christmas? Maybe I didn't mention him. He's forty and he wants to see me! I hope I can find enough to talk to him about.

FROM MARCH/

Forgive me for being such a fool. . .

Forgive me for being such a fool when you were home. I said some stupid things and I hurt you. It was after you'd gone that I came to realise the things you were saying about the full meaning of the word 'love'. You knew the whole time what it was I was scared of but I've lost my fear at last. I knew but couldn't say it, that one thing led to another from saying 'I love you' and I wasn't ready for the physical thing which came along with it. (The 'experience' last year still shocks me.) And you mustn't go on about Richard from the Red Cross. I don't want to talk about that anymore. Fullstop. For godsakes he was so old and how can I be blamed if he turns up here? Nothing 'happened'. But I agree it was odd and he's written to my parents, about 'what' I don't know and I don't care. They don't want him about the house at all. To change the subject, I've just heard the most fabulous record. I'm trying not to say 'fabulous' all the time and I'm trying hard to believe that the record is actually Australian. It's Richard Gray and the Four Brothers singing *Tina Maria*. Well, the first school social for the year was the worst the school has ever had. The Head tried and wore a dinner suit and his wife a full evening dress. He's trying to lift the tone of the school but it's hard going – when there wasn't any tone to start with. He went out the back in his bow tie and all and found two girls smoking surrounded by a mob of drunks (not school kids).

Such is life in our small town. There are rumours that the fifth year girls will be able to make their début at the Teachers' Ball. Would you come back for that or does your taking of the communists' side not let you go to débuts and balls? I do love you. Dad must realise my feelings about you because he told me I should go out with more boys and I nearly told him how I felt about you but considered it the wrong time.

FROM APRIL/
It was really great to be a 'real girlfriend'. . .
It was really great to be a 'real girlfriend' with you in the city. As much as I wanted to amaze them I didn't tell Mum and Dad about going with you to the Greek Club and the wine but I'd have loved to see Mama's reaction. I'm just dying to read your novel and glad that it's nearly finished. I thought novels took much longer (no sarcasm intended). Julia is going with Jim Fairly – don't you think that's a bit off – a fifth year girl going around with a third year boy? It wouldn't have happened in our day. Every time I get on the phone to you my heart beats like a hammer and I get hot all over and I start to perspire. This only happens before I start talking to you. As we talk I lose all these queer things and return to normal. It's almost as if I were nervous of you. But then sometimes after your calls I laugh uncontrollably and tears roll down my face and I shake. I must love you. When you come down again we must talk the matter over sanely because I don't know where we're headed. I do know we're on the edge of losing control. I'm going to get to read *East of Eden* finally (it's going the rounds). The Head put it back in the school library after Eddie gave it back as a prize. The Head has started 'Prefect Teas' where we entertain a guest. Friedman sat next to the Head's wife and Ron sat next to the Head. The Head's wife after taking a slice of cake proceeded to eat it using a teaspoon (oops, cake spoon, just to be correct) and to hide their ignorance Friedman and Ron took up their teaspoons and the whole table followed with carefully suppressed mirth unbeknownst to Mr & Mrs Head. So that's how the prefects of 1955 learned how to eat cake properly. Yes, I know your mother and

her friends eat cake with a cake fork. You still want to know the secret that I had to keep from you? You said we shouldn't have secrets from each other and that the world would be a better place without secrets. I think the world is a stranger place because of secrets. Secrets are part of being family. But I suppose you're headed towards being family. Calm down boy, not in that way, unless we have both misunderstood biology lesson 14. The secret is that Dad's father is an awful drunkard – I'm surprised you didn't know this around town – shows our families do mix in different circles. He drinks things like methylated spirits and the police are always picking him up in the town park. So you see why I worry about your drinking, especially things like whisky.

From May/
My dearest, I went to Dennis's barbecue and jitterbugged. . .
My dearest, I went to Dennis's barbecue and jitterbugged all night to get rid of my want for you. But I would like you to know that Dad picked me up at midnight and I was in bed the earliest I have ever been after a party – 1.38 being the record. Mr H. was talking to me after class and told me he once wrote a poem about love and thinking that I would appreciate it, he let me read it – the whole school seems to know about us now. The poem was beautiful and I was moved that a teacher should care about us and that he showed me something of himself. I have to say it again that I'm worried about the amount you drink and I can't keep on going along saying nothing. You've given into the stuff. You'll never be able to save or get anywhere while you drink. But there – I've said it and I'll say no more. I won't be 'nagative' again. My own confession is that I've put on weight and feel frightfully ashamed. If I'm not careful I won't fit into my new suit. Dad is always giving me money for new clothes but now he tells me at the same time to forget about boys until I'm thirty and to become a career woman. Doesn't he know that clothes are worn to attract boys? I want you to promise me that you respect me enough not to get drunk in front of me or to let me see you drunk. I don't want that ever. But when I come to the city we'll soon have your cravings under control. All the cravings (yikes!! I'm becoming outspoken!) After I've written things like this I feel so childish and old-fashioned, but I can't help it.

FROM JUNE/
Gee, I'm interested in your magazine idea. . .
Gee, I'm interested in your magazine idea and can't wait for the first
issue. Here you are just eighteen and editor of a magazine even if in
an unpaid capacity. I think it will take your mind off drink. I need to
buy some self-discipline myself – with cinemascope coming to the
little old town I'm gone for sure and will never pass the LC. *The
Student Prince* is the first cinemascope production to hit the town, an
omen, although you're no longer a student, you're still a prince, well,
just. You were a bit of a student prince you know. By the way, John,
Peter and Paul made a point of walking out of *The Angel who
Pawned her Harp* last Friday. They said they were making a protest
against unintelligent, religious films. I can't remember anyone ever
walking out of a film, can you? Who would know why they walked
out? I stayed.

I don't know why but it seems such a relief to hear you say what
the dangers of the future are for us. Now I am pretty superstitious but
as you say we are growing and likely to change mentally and
physically and now that we've had that kind of discussion it will make
us more able to accept it earlier if it happens. I told Mum that I
wanted to go to the city for the Telegraph Ball and she laughed and
said that it was too close to the exams and said "but what a ball that
is". She said the Telegraph Ball and the Arts Ball were the two most
talked about balls in Sydney. I noticed you have put both of these
down as 'musts' for us next year.

FROM JULY/
I don't offer any condolence. . .
I don't offer any condolence to you about your giving up on the novel
or for the collapse of the magazine. You mustn't think you're a failure
in life. Every time you write something it's practice for when you're
ready to do something big. For goshsakes you have a lifetime ahead
of you. Remember the American girl Jo-Anne from the Red Cross
Camp (that seems ages ago)? She writes to say that she's gone really
wild and has dyed her hair green and wears blue fingernail polish and
says she's now a 'beatnik'. We haven't any beatniks in the town yet.
We're always the last. I can't wait to read your essay on hedonism and
the reasons why the theory is incorrect and I do understand that

hedonism is not only eating and drinking. Depression again today. The thing I envy about boys, especially you, is that you can get drunk at these times. I sure felt like doing the same thing, even though I've never been drunk. Is it any wonder I get discontented though, living here in this old town while you live in Sydney and meet different people every day. Do you still keep a list of all the different sorts of people you've met? I've a question about the woman you met at a Kings Cross bar at 2.00 a.m. You said, quote and then came the inevitable 'Have you got a cigarette, pet?' end quote. Now what is the inevitable thing? You being called 'pet' (I'll call you pet in future) or being asked for a cigarette? Or am I missing something here? I talked to Friedman today and he's in a bad way. He told me he was going to leave home and drop the LC. You had better talk to him and get out of him what's wrong at home. I think I know what it is, I've felt it myself, you feel insignificant and realise that there is no way you can change the world. I know you were mad at me last weekend when you were home. You want to know why I wouldn't sit on your lap. I didn't want us to get over-excited again. Too many bouts of loving and I'm going to find myself scared stiff of you, we come too close, and my nerves can't take it.

I had a real nightmare last night. . .
I had a real nightmare last night. I kept looking for a little child who belonged to me. Every time I would find her someone would take her off me. All around the town in my dreams there were signs saying to Lane Cove trains (I've never been to Lane Cove). The washsheds, toilets and tuckshop at the school had become a railway station which trains were leaving. We assembled to join the train while I searched still for the little girl. At last I found her and we walked up Junction Street until we came to a side street and there was another sign about Lane Cove and I realised that I am to share my joy with you so I went racing up the ramp when a fellow suddenly asked me where I was going. I told him Lane Cove and he said, 'I only put that sign up to keep people away.' I started to cry and took my clothes off to keep my little girl warm. I was then left alone. Maybe all your psychology books will tell me what it means. But excuse me telling you but I felt I had to write it all down and tell you. What's the point of dreams if we can't understand them?

• • •

I'm sorry I forgot your short stories. . .

I'm sorry I forgot your short stories, but it was hard for me to know what to say about them. *City Life in Bits and Pieces* confused me. Maybe you were trying to put ideas into small parts and then fit them together to make something bigger which you hadn't planned. But I'm proud that you gave them to me to read but I feel that I have to say the truth or we will lead a life of lies. I did like the other story but somehow you made the boy superior to the girl for no good reason. He 'went cold' when the girl stood up and he discovered that her legs were in irons. That got me mad. You know I am a romanticist. And what is the mysterious story you won't show me? When will I ever 'be ready'?

FROM AUGUST/
Yes, the paper is smaller. . .

Yes, the paper is smaller and I'd hoped you wouldn't notice. I'm awful, but I have so much more work to do. After our telephone call on Friday I never expected to hear from you again. I thought for sure you would quit everything and head for Queensland to be a bum which you're always threatening to do. I knew you would get drunk too. You didn't like my last letter because I didn't write love talk. Well, school news is important to me and I didn't feel like emotionalising. I do miss you and all that but writing it down doesn't make me feel any better. I have to have a partner at the Ball and Friedman seems to be a person who wouldn't worry you. I'm reading *The Young Lions* by Irwin Shaw and it is about the last war from the German and American points of view. It is a good book but all he talks about is sex, sex, sex. I was all for realism in books until I read this. There are 665 pages and I'm up to page 255 and I can't really believe that people behave like that. I know you'll attack me for saying it but that's how I feel now. You can come home to see me as much as you like but you must understand that I am determined to study and get the LC. I think last year I was a big hindrance to you and that you would have done better. Others say that too.

Well, you've 'tested' my emotions. . .

Well, you've 'tested' my emotions with the letter 'breaking it off'.

Friedman has shown me the letter you wrote to him at the same time saying you were going to do this and for him to 'observe' me and that you were not in fact breaking it off. I take it he was only to show me the letter if I seemed to care. Well, I do care and are you satisfied? Very clever but don't try it again. I hope the gymnastics at the communist youth group take your mind off drinking. That's the good I can see in it. You may be interested in the sports carnival results, Hume first, Oxley second, Sturt third and your old house, Bass, last as usual. But it occurs to me that this must be a million miles away from you. I was stating my views about funerals at tea and I can't understand what good the words the minister says over the coffin do for the dead person. I said that we should stop having funeral services and the body should just be taken away. Mum said that the service is for the living not for the dead. For once I was at a loss. Friedman has been depressed about world events and asked Connie whether she ever got depressed. Connie thought for a while and then said, 'yes, on a wet day when I have to ride my bike to school.' Friedman was disgusted. I laughed for hours. Do you think there'll be a war? Mum does. She's been quoting the Bible a lot about war. I think I could settle it by going straight to the world leaders and asking them to wake up to themselves. I told her that you and I were going to be conscientious objectors and go to gaol together. She agreed with the idea but said she hoped they'd put us in separate cells. I am at the stage where I want to just leave school and get an ordinary job. Why does studying seem so unnatural? Gee, I'm looking forward to the party with your friends in Sydney during the holidays but I've never been to a non-school party you know. Could you find out from Richard's Jeanette just what I'm supposed to wear? Ask her if matador pants would be OK. Not having any experience of drink except half a glass of wine at the Greek Club I will leave it to your judgement what I drink. I will not have beer unless it is three parts lemonade. I'm just not used to the idea of drinking. I don't know what's come over me about people. Once upon a time I could meet anyone and not feel one least bit embarrassed but now when I know that I must be introduced to people I want to run for my life. I feel so scared about life and I don't know what I can do about it. They showed a marvellous film at Church Fellowship about atom bomb theory and how the power of the atom will help mankind. I have to keep going to Fellowship because of Mum.

• • •

FROM OCTOBER/
Boy, did the film Picnic *bring out some funny feelings. . .*
Boy, did the film *Picnic* bring out some funny feelings in me, I can't
explain them exactly, but I became practically uncontrollable when he
took his shirt off after it had been ripped, thoughts came to mind
which on a bright sunny day I would never dare to think. Dark
cinemas and films like *Picnic* should be banned. I wanted you and me
to be where there was only the two of us, somewhere where there
was no civilisation and convention. I know you think I'm dominated
by the films. It's funny I can't stay away from them and when I see
something like *Picnic* I come out of it feeling quieter with things,
except about us of course.

You really are a confidant aren't you, I wouldn't dare tell anyone
how I feel about things. Thanks for the poems of Ogden Nash. I like
him best of all the poets you've sent. Friedman, Bobby and Brian and
a couple of the other boys are behaving stupidly, skipping sport,
buying drink and going up to Big Rock to drink. In their heads
they've left school already. Stuvac begins on the 31st and there's the
school fête to be organised. Here's a rhyme for you. Mary had a little
clock, she swallowed it, it's gone, now everywhere that Mary walks,
time marches on. I got a reference from Mr L. who says that I am a
girl 'taught to observe the highest ideals with respect to morality and
general behaviour'. The kids at school think it's a classic. I'm not
going to ask for a religious reference from Rev. Benson because my
heart doesn't believe it.

I was in the Dainty-Lingerie shop this morning. . .
I was in the Dainty-Lingerie shop this morning returning something
(never mind what) and inside there was a woman buying a nightdress
and her husband was there giving approval on her selection. It was
funny to see a man doing such a thing, but they were over thirty
although only recently married. I can't describe what it was that made
me feel funny (I blushed of course). I don't know whether I want you
to choose such personal things for me, part of me says I'd like it too
much. The Head has introduced a new ceremony for fifth year –
the Passing Out ceremony (you could do that all on your own, sorry,
forgive the sarcasm). Next Monday at 9th period we assemble and a
rep. from each year will say nice things about us and then Carol and
Ron will reply and the fourth years will present us one by one with a
present, thereupon we will form a line and walk along the path and

officially pass out of the school life. I can see that it is going to be a real tear-jerker. I guessed about the 'pain' you were hinting at after your last visit home, I think it's fair that males suffer that itty bitty pain because their lives are heaven compared with the pains a woman suffers at puberty and then each month and then at motherhood. I think it's only possible to get trust between two people or a family maybe but never the world. I had a sisterly talk with Nancy and she gave me some helpful information which made me want to get to you as soon as possible. Don't ask, just wait. I said to Mr L. that there must be an easier way to get a good job than doing the LC and he said that we don't do the LC to get a job but to be educated and prepare ourselves for the person we marry. He said we should marry at our own educational level because a man and a woman have to talk to each other.

FROM NOVEMBER/
When I began to change to womanhood. . .
When I began to change to womanhood Mum gave me some books and for the first time I've seriously looked at them.

They argue that sexual relations outside marriage are wrong and they convinced me that sexual relations between us now would ruin our life. We'll cherish the feelings more once we're married. You know that it's around the school that you and I spent the Saturday night together on the train but it's now said that we 'spent the night together'. I hear your brother is worried about your family name (not my family's name). Honestly, would a child I conceived now mean the same as a child we both intended to have? I'm seeing the vocational guidance officer about advertising as a career and will put journalism second. I'm sorry if I was a wet blanket last weekend but it was my period. I believe in free love but only when the whole society believes in free love. When I'm with you and won't go the whole way I feel I'm wronging you but then I leave you and I'm nearly sick with biliousness due to nerves and the trying time we've had. I wish you would show me the story you say I'm 'not ready for' or stop referring to it all the time in such a mysterious way. At least I try to be honest with you.

The boy from the chemist's asked me out and I said yes to prove that I could go out with someone I didn't have affection for. I want

you to understand my motives. And what is this about you giving up
journalism to do a B.Sc.?

From December/
He was nice but nothing came of it. . .
He was nice but nothing came of it and it showed me that I love you
and no one measures up to you. And he is probably the last boy I will
go out with in my life. The relief that the exams are over is something
of a let–down. Our end of year party was held in Room 14. The boys
had to buy two bottles of soft drink and the girls brought a cake, I
brought a plate of pikelets. We had Sam the Gram sitting on a chair
playing all Johnny Ray, Frank Sinatra, and the Honey Brothers. All
my pikelets got eaten. We jitterbugged until 3.10 and then took the
bottles back and bought paddle pops with the refunds. Everyone
drew up their chairs and listened to the *Small One* which finished the
afternoon. We hugged each other and left the school for the last time.
There were a few tears. Speech night was more tears but with
speeches. Gee, it was a funny feeling that came over me when I
realised it was the last time I shall see many of the teachers and kids.
We are all going separate ways after five years together. It's really a
long time for a group of people to be together. I got *The Tree of Man*
and Somerset Maugham's *Short Stories Volume One*. No Steinbeck
this year. Friedman didn't wear a blazer and he had to go up for the
softball cup. In his back pocket was Plato, the biggest Penguin ever
printed. The Head gave a speech and most of us cried. Today I was
cleaning my room getting rid of old school books from five years. I
burned everything except some prac. notes that I might need if I have
to sit the LC again. The town is dead and now every time I walk by
Ted's milk bar he looks out and smiles at me really wistfully. There
are only young kids hanging around there now. The old gang is gone.
I have to iron all my clothes that I'm taking with me to Sydney on
Friday. I realise that this will be the last letter I ever have to write
from the old town to you. It's become a habit, I think I'm going to
miss doing it. I love you very much my darling and I'm very proud
that you love me.

• THE STORY NOT SHOWN •

Tony pushed his half-empty glass across the bar, said, 'I can't finish this.' I drained mine. Tony was not too keen on beer but for a fellow not too keen on beer he swallowed a large enough amount. The barman shouted, 'Hurry along please.' and we left. I would estimate that we were three-quarters drunk. But it is hard to estimate. I considered myself less drunk than Tony. I know that my mind was criticising some of Tony's talk although I wasn't expressing my criticism. I was saying to myself, 'You're drunk Tony, you're drunk boy.' Tony was speaking about his favourite writer, Hemingway. Hemingway said war is a good thing because no writer is experienced without experiencing a war. Tony was also saying corny things about journalism like, 'It's a tough game we're in, Ian.'

We went to a coffee shop. Over coffee Tony told me how a Jew had killed his father. The Jew had thrown a hand grenade during an army exercise. The grenade had bounced off the tree and landed at his father's feet and exploded.

He'd told me this before.

'Damn it, Ian, we have to have experience.'

I agreed.

'Let's find ourselves a couple of whores.'

I was inwardly surprised. It was the last thing I expected from Tony, who had a girlfriend.

I said that I didn't have enough money.

He said he had enough for both of us.

I said it was all right by me.

So we went to Kings Cross. I had an idea that we would not find any prostitutes. Tony was walking determinedly, talking of Hemingway and the need to 'experience' life.

William Street was full of commercial brightness. Advertising beauty formed by gas-filled tubes and electricity.

We turned off William Street and went along narrow dark alleys.

We passed a man who said, 'Along there, mate,' and indicated a lane.

We turned into that lane.

A few houses had lights on. The lights from the houses revealed little groups of men at the doors of the depressing tenement houses. The men were quiet, some leaning with hands in pockets, some walking back and forth. They did not seem to be talking. I also noticed in some doorways women leaning sardonically against the doors. The street was so dim that it was hard to distinguish any particulars.

I went up to a woman at the doorway and said, 'How much?'

Her old voice said, 'Three quid for a few minutes or five quid for a strip.'

A little voice in my head said, 'This is it, mate.'

Tony had the money, so he accepted. Before he went in I asked him for three quid. He had to ask the prostitute for change. They went in, the door shut and a few minutes later the door opened again and Tony passed out three quid to me. The prostitute said, 'You can go somewhere else or wait till your mate is finished.' I said I would go somewhere else.

I wandered along past a group of men. I somehow thought that the larger the group the better the prostitute, but didn't feel like waiting for ten or fifteen minutes while they all finished.

I went up to a woman in a doorway.

'How much?'

'Sorry love, I'm not working tonight.'

I walked on.

Up to another woman. She told me three pounds.

There were no lights on in the house. We went inside.

The woman switched on a feeble light in the corner. It showed a bare room with a double bed. The bedspread looked dirty.

'Sit on the chair and take off your coat,' she said.

I did so.

'Righto, undo your fly.' I did so.

She produced a basin of water and roughly washed my penis.

Though drunk I summed the woman up as ugly, fat and degenerate. But for the alcohol she would have appeared repulsive.

But she appeared to me as only one thing - woman.

She rolled her fat body onto the bed with a practised movement and pulled her skirts up. What was revealed did not seem pretty. I lay on top of her. She exposed her breasts. She grunted in a hard voice and I could not tell whether this was only sound-effects or genuine expressions of effort.

After a while she said, 'Are you coming yet?' I was too drunk to feel much sexual excitement but I came.

'OK, get off, I can tell you're finished.'

She washed me and switched off the light and showed me to the door.

I said, 'How are the tough economic conditions affecting you?'

I was trying to sound friendly and nonchalant.

She replied, 'It don't worry me, love, I only do this while me husband is away. Mind the step.'

I found myself out in the dark, wet street. I could not believe what I had done. I shouted for Tony and he came out of the darkness.

He had a black fellow with him. Tony explained that the black fellow had been refused by one of the prostitutes.

I was angered. The three of us went up to the prostitute and I said, 'Don't you believe in the United Nations? Why don't you let our friend in?'

She snarled, ' Take him home to your sister or mother.'

Tony said, 'You dirty slut.'

I held Tony back.

He was shouting about colour bars and sluts. The black fellow and I dragged Tony away. The prostitute shouted, 'Keep him away from here or he will have a pistol in his ribs.''

Tony cooled down. The black fellow said he was from the Solomon Islands. He said, 'Why is it, you have a heart, I have a heart, you have blood and I have blood, but because of my skin she hates me.'

'I don't know, mate,' Tony said.

The black fellow then started talking about God, love, kindness and King David, in a deep, soft native voice and broken English.

He worked on a boat. Tony wrote his telephone number on a piece of paper and gave it to him saying, 'If you're ever in trouble call this number at the Daily Mirror.'

We left him walking up and down the street offering prostitutes his money and being refused.

Tony said, 'What's wrong with the world, mate, what's wrong with it?'

He was still slightly drunk. I shook my head but did not reply. I was thinking about VD.

• BEIRUT •

After London, Edith and he had to join up for an official visit to a research reactor in Israel. In Tel Aviv, they again had an argument about sight–seeing in Jerusalem – he didn't want to go there.

'I can't believe you would pass it up,' she said, 'given that Merrick has so kindly laid it on.'

'I was filled with mumbo–jumbo about religion and Jerusalem when I was a kid, it makes me feel sick even now. I can still see the coloured prints of deserts, donkeys, palm trees, camels, crowns of thorns and whatever on the Sunday School wall. As a kid I felt that a religion coming from that sort of country and from people dressed like that could have nothing to do with me. I *knew* it could have nothing to do with me.'

'Except that it laid the basis for our laws and ethics,' Edith said, primly.

'It wasted the Sundays of my childhood when I should've been out in the bush.'

He drank his beer and looked out on the Mediterranean and he felt a regurgitation of all the feelings he'd had back in that country–town Sunday School. What did it have to do with his friends? With the pushy, talkative ten-year-old Robyn whom he'd later married? Sin and death and bodies anointed with oil.

'I simply fail to see how Sunday School experiences would prevent you as a grown man from sight-seeing in an ancient city like Jerusalem.' She again looked hurt about his refusal to be her companion. 'After all, I'm a humanist myself.'

That at seventy she should use a label like that seemed inappropriate. She was an eminent woman with honours, a reputation, she didn't need a single label. But during the mission with him he'd noticed she'd used labels like that, perhaps to draw attention away from a generalised image of 'eminent old woman' towards more vigorous identities belonging to her fierce, fervent youth. For a seventy-year-old she was youthfully passionate about environmental concerns, although being with him had caused her to act with less piety because of his joking irreverence about such things, but in fact they were not wide apart in politics, just style.

'You're drinking more,' she said, 'not that it's any of my business.'

He stared back at her. She sometimes drove him to anger but there were those moments, like their shared cognac in the evening before saying goodnight and going to their own rooms, to which he now looked forward. Especially against the daily changing scenes and faces, their relentless itinerary. They had become for each other a familiar fixed domestic point.

'It's Marlowe doing this to you,' she said playfully, picking up the book from the table, 'reading too much about the tragic history of the life and death of Doctor Faustus. You're frightened you'll meet the Devil in Jerusalem.'

'Who will offer me a deal too good to refuse? No, Edith, I can't really face Jerusalem even if there's the chance of a deal. Too much Sunday School.'

'Never heard of anything more ridiculous from a grown man.'

Edith went to Jerusalem with the First Secretary from the Australian Embassy while he drank bloody marys in the King David Lounge, the first decent bloody mary he'd had on the trip, and considered the biblical references around him – including his drink, he silently laughed at the biblical connection. As ever he pondered his personal losses and the incompleteness of his life, his doubts about his contract with the department being renewed.

What he really wanted to do was to go to Lebanon and the civil war there. He wanted to peer into the abyss. Maybe go into the abyss. The IAEA work was too paleface – he wanted to be a redskin.

He watched two young uniformed Israelis, a woman and a man, both with their Uzi machine guns, holding hands as they walked into the Hilton restaurant. They hung their guns over the backs of their chairs. They chattered animatedly.

Gun-fighting politics was no more real than the committee room. Or the political theory class. But why then did it *seem* different, not only in degree but qualitatively?

He saw them studying the menu. He hoped they could afford whatever they wanted from it. Sometimes he wanted to pay for the young to have whatever they wanted in life. He hated to be in a queue for, say, opera or theatre and hear young people ahead of him being unable to afford the tickets.

He wanted to be shot. That was what he wanted. The fourth bloody mary said that to him. He'd had enough. He'd cut his toenails too many times. He wasn't good at living. He didn't do it right. Living made him uncomfortable.

He turned his attention to two young Israeli women showing each other their credit cards. He liked the way they were celebrating their professional status and whatever the cards said about their self-performance. Their economic prowess.

He was impatient for Edith to return from Jerusalem.

He rang one of his two friends in the Israeli Defence Force and inquired about getting up to Beirut.

Yizhar was encouraging and said he'd try to arrange something.

When he returned from the telephone he found Edith saying goodbye to the First Secretary.

'How was it?' he asked. 'Let me get you both a drink.'

Merrick excused himself but Edith sat down tiredly.

'Given your feelings about Jerusalem, I shouldn't tell you about it.' she said, flushed from the trip. 'It was just as you feared I suppose, and just as I'd hoped.'

'Good.'

'And I took a decision,' she said, 'in the historic city of Jerusalem I took a personally historic decision.'

He looked at her inquiringly.

'Yes. I stood on Mount Scopus and decided to leave my husband.'

She was seventy and he'd forgotten the husband. She was the public figure, her husband was not.

But another thought strayed in – had *he* played some part in this decision? No. Not possible.

'May I ask why? Why Mount Scopus? Did that play a part?

Haven't you been married for some time? Sorry   –   a few questions tangled up there.'

'This is my second marriage. But Richard and I have been together twenty-seven years.'

'That's, well, a long time.'

'Yes.'

She drank the Scotch straight down. He beckoned the waiter for another.

'It came about on the telephone last night. He said that the last three years had been the happiest of his life. I was dumbfounded. I felt they had been a steep decline into sourness. I hadn't thought he would see the marriage so differently from the way I saw it. I couldn't believe he had not noticed *my* condition. Or that I hadn't noticed how *he* felt. The complete delusion into which both of us had sunk.'

She didn't have the tone of voice which suggested she wanted counselling. How could someone like him with such a lousy personal track record counsel a seventy-year-old anyhow, especially one coming out of a twenty-seven-year marriage?

'I'm really a very solitary person,' she said.

He didn't believe that.

'I find it hard to say anything,' he said, 'too far outside my jurisdiction.'

'I don't really, at my age, seek advice. But I do need someone to, well, *say it to*. Just for the confidence which comes from hearing the words uttered. To put them out there into the world for all to see.'

'Of course.'

'Do you know what we argued about most?'

He gave a small shake of his head to encourage and yet to avoid showing a prying interest.

'Health   –   and how the body functions. I'm not a food faddist, regardless of what you think.'

He didn't think she was a faddist. She seemed to eat her way through the food of any nationality. Give or take a few normal sorts of prejudices.

'Throughout our married life he held to five incorrect understandings of how the body worked. I myself no longer believe we are what we eat. The body seems to me to be remarkably adaptable and tolerant and forgiving, and capable of all sorts of corrections and absorptions and rejuvenations.'

He had a feeling she'd said this many times in arguments with her husband. She pursued the subject.

'And we seem to have a palate which invites indulgence. I know some lovable gluttons and some highly productive and happy people with absolutely horrible diets and I know, on the other hand, some dreadfully grim people with terribly correct diets. Oh, I observe the basic rules, but as I've grown older I've said "what the hell". He was so wrong about the function of the kidneys for instance. But. . . ' she stopped as though hearing herself and realising she was going beyond the boundaries of the conversational territory. Explaining her husband's view of anatomy was going too far.

'We seem to use food to exorcise demons,' he mumbled, to cover her embarrassment. 'Trying to bring about personal revolution by dietary upheaval. Eating is play too.' He trailed off.

'No, I'm leaving him when I return. I'll get by all right. I don't think my diet will alter anything.'

She was drifting into an introspective appraisal of her life.

They sat quietly for a while with their drinks.

At breakfast next day Yizhar, his Israeli army friend, came in in uniform, grinning, hearty. He was the only Israeli who seemed to have a properly tailored uniform. He carried the rank of colonel.

After coffee and convivialities Yizhar said to him, 'You want to see Beirut. It's madness up there, you know.'

'Oh that's interesting,' Edith cut in, 'I was in Beirut – well, the year doesn't matter – before the war, the Second World War, that is, I'd really love to see it again.' She looked at him, 'I hope I'm included in your sight-seeing plans this time?'

'I wouldn't call it sight-seeing,' Yizhar said, breaking into deep laughter.

No and no, he had not included her in his plans. They were getting along better and he had not seen her going with him into Beirut. Perhaps it diluted the macho image he had of 'going into Beirut.' Or maybe her natural or whatever presence was a shield which he did not want given his present life tiredness.

'It's a bit rough up there Edith – there's a civil war going on. One of us should stay behind to tell the tale.'

The look she gave him implied a belittling offence against her as a friend, or as a woman, or as an older person.

'I've been in tough places and done what would be considered rather dangerous things in my time,' she said, shortly, and her eyes then slipped away from conversational focus to a bright reflective glaze. 'Oh yes, Beirut before the war wasn't all that safe either, though I dare say it was much safer than it is now. But I carried a revolver then. I had to fire shots, I remember, even then, some intruder or bandit. A bomb was thrown. A grenade.'

Edith no longer surprised him.

'The Kit Kat Club,' Yizhar said, 'you were there in the days of the glittering Beirut.'

'Oh yes, but for me it was the Club St George and the Colorado.'

'What were you doing there, Edith? Apart from living it up?' he asked.

'I was with the League of Nations – a very junior technical officer, nothing important. But you must really find a place for me on your trip.'

Yizhar seemed not to be dismayed by the idea. 'I'll arrange it, but. . .' he shrugged, grinned, 'all care; no responsibility. Invisibly official, you'll be. If you know what I mean. If I know what I mean.'

'Oh, I don't expect to find my Beirut of course, but it will bring back memories.'

'No, your Beirut it won't be.'

'I came across from Paris on the old Orient Taurus Express – all those frontier checks.'

'We'd better take our hip flasks, Edith, the Colorado is probably closed.'

In his bed the next morning he awoke and met the familiar emotional condition which settled on him before every expedition of his adult life. It was a numbed control. There was none of the nervous excitement of childhood. He knew he was over–controlled but that no effort of will could break him free from that. His mind, as he lay there, sensibly prepared lists, rehearsed for exigencies. As he showered he looked at ways the day might possibly go; he would have made a good staff officer. But he had a yearning to be able to enter experience thoughtlessly, to be able to expose himself without armour or caution – to deal with exigencies as they arrived with what was at hand, to meet the world with surprise and then to perform in ways that surprised him. He knew that when such situations did crash in on him in life he performed well, but his pre-planned, pre-rehearsing mind meant that things rarely crashed in on him. He wanted more emergencies in his life. His nervousness, too, caused the essence of so many experiences to elude him, so much of his living had essence only as recall.

As he packed his SW band radio in case 'all hell breaks loose and we are pinned down for days and don't know what's going on', he filled his pockets with Palfium and packed penicillin and tranquillisers. He filled his hip flask and put his Swiss army knife in his pocket.

But I am this sort of person, he said aloud to himself as he stood there in his room at the Hilton, running through his mental check list. I am a survivor. Maybe he had to be that sort of person to survive the irregularities of his personal emotional life, the rootlessness.

His young ex-girlfriend in London had once said she admired his 'completeness' after he had told her that he had finally got some things right in his life, his clothes, his travelling gear, his filing system. He handled his job well. He enjoyed the accoutrements of living, being properly equipped to face life. But he had confined his personal estate, he had no family, no major possessions. Even so, he felt that this pared-down existence, this confined estate, was still fragile, was on the verge of escaping his control.

In the car on the road to Beirut, Yizhar said, 'I have to repeat that this is dangerous country. Although we are in a non-military vehicle, even though we are staying in the Christian zone - it is still dangerous.' Yizhar was out of uniform but on the floor on the passenger's side was an Uzi and a two-way radio.

They passed an occasional armoured personnel carrier, now and then a tank, they saw displaced persons riding on the top of their possessions on the backs of trucks - a now-familiar photographic image from many wars.

On this visit to Europe he had wanted to go to Spain with his young girlfriend. He had wanted to seek out the traces of the Spanish Civil War and to play out the film *The Passenger* and perhaps to die in the Hotel de la Gloria. Now he thought, I am in another civil war, and I might die here, instead.

'Beirut was named after Julia Augusta Berytus, the Roman emperor's daughter, 64 BC. She was licentious,' Yizhar said in the voice of a tour guide.

'Oh yes,' Edith said with a rush, delighting in her recollection, 'she got into trouble with Augustus, didn't she. I seem to think he banished her. Because of her behaviour.'

'Something like that,' said Yizhar.

'I'm rather pleased I remembered that,' Edith said.

Had his great–grandmother been licentious? He was glad that he was offering himself up to death in a city named after a licentious woman.

He wondered about Edith and her youth as a technical officer for the League of Nations in Beirut, living in the hotel district on the Avenue de Paris as she had described it. Dancing at night clubs. Was she wild? And in Spain as Ascaso's mistress – or just friend, she hadn't been clear on that.

The bad thing was to be living but diminished by not wanting to be living. If you lived, you should live to the full, he'd always tried to do that. Either live fully or die. He was not good at living. He lived out of a swag. He had no centre. Today he was just as curious about death as he was about whatever living had to offer up ahead. He stared out at the windows of the worn and damaged buildings, welcoming any bullet which might spurt from them. He enjoyed the stark seriousness at least of having an Uzi machine gun on the floor at his feet. The two–way radio messages coming and going in flat Hebrew. He picked up the Uzi.

'I hope you know about guns if you are going to play about with it.' Yizhar said.

'I know a bit about guns,' he said, 'I did basic army training.'

'It's the guns that I don't like about all this,' Edith said.

He put the Uzi back on the floor at his feet.

'I would, however, like to hold it for a moment,' Edith said.

He turned to Yizhar who said to her, without taking his eyes from the road, 'Just don't touch the trigger, Edith.'

'Oh I won't do anything silly.'

He picked up the Uzi and carefully handed it over to Edith in the back.

He remembered a party in his youth in Australia when Turvey had shot off a round from a Bren gun. He laughed to himself now about the hysterics of that evening. He told Yizhar and Edith the story. But now parties were predictable because infinite promise had gone from their lives. Turvey back then was forever preparing for revolution. Now he owned a computer software company.

Negotiation had become the adventure of his life now. Negotiation over the wording of a preambular paragraph, the annexure, the attachment, the operative paragraphs – recalls, considers, affirms, concerned, aware, expresses, urges, declares, requests.

'Of all the weapons, the machine gun is most full of evil intent,' Edith said, handing back the gun.

'I like firing machine guns,' he said. 'Do you like it?' he asked Yizhar.

'Not particularly. I see it as a desperate sort of weapon. Firing away all that lead in wild hope of hitting something.'

They passed through Sidon, where bulldozers were pushing garbage into the sea.

Yizhar's hand was on the horn almost constantly, moving aside people and animals who moved but did not bother to look at the car.

'Of course when I was here before the war,' Edith went on, 'I never got down to the south – we went to the mountains. Now when I see it all in such disarray I feel we are falling backwards into history.'

Yizhar stopped the car. 'You drive,' he said, getting out of the car and giving him the driver's seat. 'I'd better ride shotgun for a while. Remember, no matter what happens keep driving. There are no traffic police here. Rules, none.' Yizhar took out a map.

Guided by Yizhar he drove the car into Beirut.

They had reached the green line which divided the Christian and Muslim sectors when a shot sounded and shooting began somewhere nearby. Despite the uselessness of the action, both he and Yizhar ducked involuntarily at the sound of the first shot.

'Keep driving,' Yizhar said, 'whatever happens don't stop.'

Then a thud and a crack of the windscreen shattering at the back.

'We're hit.'

'Keep on going,' Yizhar said, gesturing south, bending down and taking up the Uzi which he cocked clumsily with none of the practised ease of an infantry man.

The firing receded behind them.

'You OK Edith?' he said, and he and Yizhar looked around, he fleetingly, returning his eyes to the road, having registered though that Edith was not all right, was slumped in her seat. 'Shall I stop – has she fainted? Is she OK?'

'You keep driving, I'll look,' and Yizhar rolled himself over into the back seat.

'All right,' he said, 'stop.'

'Is she hit?'

'No – I don't think so.'

Yizhar with Uzi in hand looked out and around the area. 'Pull over against that wall.'

He looked at Edith who was still unconscious, unmoving.

Yizhar handed the Uzi to him. 'Shoot anything that seems hostile. I think it's her heart. She isn't hit. But she's dead. She's gone.' He was working on her chest.

'Dead?'

'Afraid so.'

'Let's get the hell out of here,' Yizhar said, 'there's nothing I can do. We'll be better off back in Israel.'

'She's really dead?'

'Oh yes.'

He looked down at her: but Edith, I was the one who wanted to go, you've got my bullet. But go with God, Edith. Or go with the universe you cared for.

'She was seventy.'

'She seemed to have lived well enough,' Yizhar said, 'but go, go.'

'Yes,' he said, starting the car, pulling back onto the road, suppressing the shaking which was moving through him, 'she probably did. She was going to leave her husband.'

He pulled out the hip flask. 'You want a shot?' he asked Yizhar.

Yizhar shook his head, 'I'll wait till I get back to the safety of the Hilton.'

He decided to wait as well and put the hip flask back in his bag.

Yizhar's hand nervously patted the dash. 'I'll have some paperwork to do. Thank God she wasn't killed by gunshot. We'll avoid an inquiry. I'll have to fiddle place of death. You might have to do false swearing.'

'Sure.'

'I have friends at hospital. We'll be OK.'

'She could just as well have died on a flight of stairs.'

Yizhar nodded. They drove back in virtual silence, not commenting on the urine and excreta smells coming from Edith.

He had a dreadful feeling that he might have to live out the rest of his life, that somehow an early death had been taken from him – this was a nonsensical way of thinking, but as Louise had once said to him, 'You have to decide whether to take omens or not to take omens.' He had never decided whether to take them or not. Or whether reversing omens was a way of taking them too.

'Were you close to her?' Yizhar asked after a time.

'In an odd way we were becoming closer. We'd been thrown together by this delegation.'

He would have to talk to her husband. And to the government. And probably the news media back in Australia. She was an eminent person.

'I was prejudiced against her at first – probably because of her age. But she was also very earnest – she lightened up as we went on. I seem though to have such a small reaction to her death. Sad, but not dramatically sad.'

He told Yizhar that he'd heard of the death of his former wife from cancer while he'd been in Vienna. He had not been satisfied by his reactions to her death either. His reactions had seemed somehow deficient.

'I think we expect culturally to be awed and stunned and so on by it. But generally we aren't. I think it's normal with someone not close to us to feel nothing.'

Nothing to be said. Nothing to be known. Nothing to be felt.

He found himself smiling at the recollection of Edith helping with a trick in Vienna that they'd played on the Russian delegate.

Remembering too the drunken night in Vienna when late at night in her room their eyes had met with fleeting, hopelessly inappropriate carnal intent. Remembering her naked. Remembering the optical illusion of seeing his girlfriend's face in Edith's in the art gallery.

• EX–WIFE RE–WED •

She did not tell him herself, Louise told him with that status of voice used for information or gossip of profound content – 'Did you hear about Robyn?'

He noticed that Louise did not use their usual expression 'ex–wife'. Robyn had not been known as anything else but 'ex–wife' since they divorced – Jesus Christ, was it really fifteen years ago – and she remarried. She had become again the person 'Robyn' not just the 'ex–wife' character in Louise's and his conversation.

'Well? Tell me.'

How would Louise have heard anything of Robyn, who now lived in Portugal and who moved in a different world?

'It's the Big C.'

The Big C. Louise's voice was enlivened by her role as the bearer of grim news, by being able to dance death into their lives.

Louise was one of the few of his current friends who had known the 'marriage'.

'How did you hear?' He wanted to know how she knew and he did not – given that neither of them was any longer in contact with Robyn.

'Purely by chance,' Louise said. 'I was in Lyon at a trade exhibition when I met her.'

'Does she say I gave her the cancer?' It was a joking toughness to block the shock and the pity which were reaching him. 'She blamed me for everything else.' Louise managed a small laugh, it was their style of humour not Robyn's style of humour. 'How bad is it, Louise?'

'Bad. Irreversible.'

Next day there was an uninformative overseas call from Robyn on his answering machine. The first contact for years. He did not telephone but wrote a letter which told her he knew about her illness and which like all other exchanges since they'd broken was another effort to discharge the guilt he felt about their time together. A fading guilt, and an unfairly borne guilt, given that they'd married as teenagers. At times of low spirit, though, he still felt it was he who'd failed, who'd broken the vows. Of course it wasn't like that, but at these low times he felt he should have stayed with the marriage despite the incompatibility which had shown early up. Would he have been any the worse off? Maybe he would have been anchored enough to become a writer when he'd mistakenly thought he would need to be unanchored. He was still plagued by how she'd crashed their bright red car on the third day they'd had it and he'd yelled at her, failed to comfort her. It was their first significant possession, a materialisation of their relationship. He should have comforted her; instead, he yelled at her. Or was she unconsciously crashing their relationship? As a callow husband he'd attacked her for feeling pre-menstrual tension. He had read to her from a book which said it was 'all in the mind'. He had forced her to admit that it was 'all in the mind' and to pretend she suffered nothing.

His letter to her was short, he said he'd heard she was ill and he was willing her recovery and rooting for her with all his spirit, which he was. Rooting was an odd word for him to have settled on, in their country-town school days it had been fucking. He pondered this and then left the word in the letter.

He said that for his part he remembered good times and rich moments from when they'd been young kids going into life together. He said he still suffered too from things he'd handled badly. He mentioned their 'farcical reunion' a few years earlier.

She wrote back saying how affected she was to get a letter and that she too certainly carried good memories in her heart and had since laughed about their 'farcical reunion'.

Their daughter whom he'd never known was now at university in the States.

She said she was returning to Australia and hoped he'd be in the country and able to see her and that it would not be a second 'farcical' reunion.

After a boozy night with old friends at the Journalists' Club he drove her back to their home town which was no longer a town so much as a suburb of a city.

'We should call it "the suburb" I suppose, not the "old town",' she said.

'I guess we still see the *town*.'

'I can still feel the town.'

She had lost much weight but still seemed agile and he still saw in her the movements of the girlish hockey player. She gave off what he saw as a strained cheeriness and he had not mentioned her cancer and neither had she. He didn't feel he should raise it, sensing it to be perhaps anti-therapeutic to acknowledge it or that cancer was something best handled with hauteur rather than candour.

'The old school is really now the *old* school,' he said, 'as old as anything ever gets in this ever-renewing country.'

'Yes,' she said, 'let's go to the school. I'd like to see the old school again.'

He felt the unspoken part of her sentence.

'Remember planting those trees in the new school when we were prefects?' she said, as they sat in the car looking at the row of eucalyptus trees which they'd planted, now well grown – twenty-five-years old. The summer wind gave them a green-silver light and the leaves seemed to shake, frustratedly, against the unmoving solidity of the trunk and limbs. The trees took him back to before high school, to the primary school and hot endless days when she and he had been children in the playground, hot and breathless, aware of each other but unable to express or understand this uncomfortable awareness, only able to express it finally by chasing, hair-pulling, tickling.

'A penny for them.'

They had been going so well and now she'd come out with one of those detestable phrases which he remembered once made up so much of her conversation. Her intelligent ordinariness had enraged him back then. During adolescence he'd fought against what he'd seen then as the tyranny of ordinariness and the tyranny of convention. He'd used excessive behaviour, flamboyance borrowed from literature, self-dramatisation, rule-breaking, bohemian posing, all as resistance to, and inoculation against, the ordinariness of his country-town life. He'd laid down rules for his friends' conversation at high school – no clichés, no wishing people good luck, no salutations, no greetings. And now, even near her death he couldn't let her get away with it, out it came.

'I don't know what I was thinking but I'm now thinking about how we tried to ban those sorts of expressions when we were here at school.'

'What sorts of expressions?!'

'Oh, sayings like, "a penny for them".' He felt foolish for having made the point.

'Oh God yes, so you did.'

He was trying to be light but somewhere there in him was the adolescent trying to remake the world, to impose his own minor tyrannies. He hoped she didn't sense it. Back then she'd always been praised for her 'common sense', for being 'down to earth'. He'd been striving for an 'uncommon sense'. His models then were artists, revolutionaries, dreamers – none of which he'd become, becoming instead a servant of an international agency, practising mundane idealism, circumscribed dreaming, deferred dreaming, the illusions of a negotiated revolution. He turned again to her, recalling that along with the down-to-earthness she had also believed in some non-rational things, the meaning in coincidence, the usefulness of astrology. But what about his own White Knight plague of coincidences which had swept through his life that year? He smiled to himself, unable to reveal it to her. He still had to set an example for her, as he had tried to do back in high school, as the relentless rationalist. He then wondered fleetingly if she really did have cancer or whether this was a mid-life panic, had she really been diagnosed or was it some sort of intuitive self-diagnosis? She was capable of that.

'Yes,' she said, 'you didn't want people to say hello or goodbye, it wasted time, we were to speak only if we had something to say worth saying or truly felt. Yes. And everything had to be "original".' She snorted.

'I was a bit of a zealot.'

'You sure were.'

This hurt, he didn't want her to confirm that, he didn't think he'd been a zealot. 'Did you really all think I was a zealot?'

'Oh yes. There was lots of talk about you. You were always trying to make the school – or our year – into some sort of branch of the Communist Party or a commune or whatever it was you were reading at the time. *Walden.* Maybe not a zealot but a very, very serious boy. Maybe that's why I married you.'

He remembered that it was back then that he'd had to confront his first sad misconception about the world. He'd wanted to believe that his friends at school were true students, his teachers true scholars, all concerned only with inquiry. That all adults respected truth and the weight of evidence.

This misconception still caught him out, still took root in his mental garden and, of course, was still the fallacy he had to work by.

'You were pretty queer,' she said, 'but impressive in your own way.' She pushed his arm playfully. 'Don't look so worried – we didn't think you were a loony. We were more worried that you would think we were dumb. Did you think I was dumb back then?'

'I married you. You got a better pass than I did.'

'We know that examinations don't count in the long run. Did you think I wasn't an intellectual? And anyhow men marry women dumber than themselves for security.'

'I was sometimes driven up the wall by your common sense. You saw through all the bullshit.'

But she was never sure what was really bullshit and she had neither insight nor vision.

He laughed. 'I miss it now and then. We need you in Vienna.' He didn't believe that.

She asked about schoolfriends, Carl, Sylvia, Friedman. 'Do you ever hear from them?'

'No, not at all really. Sylvia's with the Schools Commission. She's always being written up in those articles on successful feminist women.'

'Sounds just like her.'

Sounds just like her.

'Let's go into the school.'

They got out of the car. It was vacation. The school was empty. Nothing as empty as a vacant school.

'Let's go to Room 14. The Prefects' Room.'

He was thinking of another room, where they had almost made love for the first time. Room 17?

'Why not Room 17?'

She turned to him smiling, almost a blushing smile. 'Of course, I'd almost forgotten that. Oh yes.'

They walked along the corridors, the smell of chalk, always oranges? or fruit-cake? Or were these smells in his mind?

They stopped and looked into Room 17, the art room. She took his hand and squeezed it.

'We came very close,' she said.

'The Gestetner's been replaced by offset.'

They went on to Room 14 where the flirtings, the brushings, the illicit hand-holding, the supercharged touchings of pre-courtship, had begun.

The room was crowded with superseded household appliances, jugs, toasters, heaters, snack-makers.

'They have more electrical gadgets than we had.'

'We had a jug – for instant coffee – they've got a restaurant-style dripolator.'

She leaned into him affectionately. 'You wrote a story for the school magazine about nuclear war beginning the day you got your examination results – remember? And you end up being involved in all that even now.'

'Not quite "all that", but yes, that's where I ended up.'

'Though now you're for using nuclear power aren't you?'

'Only because it's inescapable for the time being.'

'But you were aware of the threat before other people.'

'Not really.'

'Before *we* were at school. You were a peace movement before there were peace movements.'

'What it shows twenty-five years later is that I was politically wrong – the bomb hasn't dropped – maybe it stopped war.'

He realised he was slightly disturbed by her holding his hand; it was, he realised, irritation with himself, a fear of contact with her. Because she had cancer. He was angry with himself and took her other hand against this stupid gut reaction.

'I think I was using it metaphorically – the bomb.'

This idea seemed to be unacceptable to her. 'How? Why?'

'I think I was really writing about the bomb of puberty dropping on the peace of my childhood.'

'I don't think you were. I don't think you were that clever.' She laughed to avoid any offence.

He let go of her hands and went to the window to look across at the playing field. She came up behind him and embraced him from behind, her cheek coming against his. Again he felt a resistance to her but suppressed it.

'You haven't mentioned my cancer,' she said. She tried to say it in a comic voice but it threw a shadow of effort. 'For godsake, mention my cancer,' she laughed, and going to the window, opened it and shouted, 'Cancer!' and then closed it. 'There, it's mentioned. People won't mention it. I didn't think it would happen with you and me but it has. People won't say the word. But I *have* to talk about it.'

The effort at lightness was so colossal and so transparent and courageous he felt tearful.

'You look so well – it hadn't crossed my mind,' he said, holding his voice normal, 'but OK – how's the cancer going?'

His voice came out far from normal.

She made physical contact with him again, leaning into him. 'Oh I have my winning days and my losing days. It's incredible that I can really say at the end of a day – I'm winning or I'm losing. But I'm not strong enough to count the winning days against the losing days. That's where I'm a sook. But I'm not a defeatist.'

She had never been a defeatist. But the word sounded too close to being crushingly, inescapably upon her. She stumbled over saying it.

'Does it hurt a lot?'

'Hellishly in the lower pelvis sometimes.'

'I've heard that chemotherapy is rough.'

'Oh I've given that up. I didn't believe that anything that makes you feel that bad could be good for you.'

'Louise said you were having Cobalt 60 inter-cavity irradiation.'

'Yes, but I gave it up.'

'But why, Robyn, why?'

She squeezed his hand. 'Don't feel offended because your magic is being refused.'

It wasn't *his* magic – nor was it 'magic'.

'I changed therapies,' she said, 'as Susan Sontag said, all the medical therapies are like warfare – they bombard, they attack, they search out and destroy.'

'But for godsake, Robyn, they *work*.'

'Calm down, calm down. So does my way.'

Her way.

'I'm meditating and I have a vegan diet which is all I feel like eating anyhow – now hold on – don't be so quick to make a mock of it. It works too, you know. I'm doing imagery therapy – the Simonton technique.'

'The what!'

'Calm down. I imagine the white cells eating the cancer, as simple as that. I believe in the power of the imagination. But I don't see it as a violent act – I imagine it as peaceful. The imagination is a much under-used power.'

She looked very tired from having had to put it into words against her sense of his opposition. She had stated it as a testament of faith. Oh he was still so zealous with her. He angered again against himself. He wanted to take both her hands and kiss them as a supportive gesture and as a way of dissenting from those negative responses his personality was giving to her. But still he could not bring himself to do it.

'You're not looking like an invalid,' he forced himself to say, 'so something's working, maybe.' He tried to bite back the word 'maybe'. 'I'm sorry I mocked you – you know me, always the schoolboy rationalist.'

'But a rationalist who was sophisticated would accept that there are these grey areas in medicine and especially in cancer healing. Strange things do happen.'

'Yes. I'm for anything that works for you,' he said, feeling happier with that form of words, 'but why don't you try everything at once? The Cobalt 60, the alternative therapies, the lot.'

'But don't you see that if you try the medical things you're being passive – you're putting yourself in the hands of other people and saying "cure me". With the other therapies you are active – it's me working for my own cure.'

But there was nothing in the book that said you shouldn't put yourself in the hands of others when ill. Trusting, or involving others, might be part of being committed to your life. He didn't want to argue with her. He was afraid of upsetting the balance of her will, in so far as he was granting validity to willpower cures. He suspected, though, that do-it-yourself cures might be a diseased reaction to disease. We could not depend upon the beneficence of the unconscious. He wouldn't rely on his.

'Remember that last party we had here at the end of fifth year,' she said, 'no, of course, you were already in Sydney. We had my old gramophone here,' she went over and stood where the gramophone had been, 'we drank soft drinks and ate cakes which the girls had baked.' She stood in reverie. 'Gee. . .' She became tearful.

He wanted to go to her but the resistance was still there.

They traced their school lives slowly as they wandered about the empty school.

'I was truly deeply shocked that day in Room 17. I mean, I hadn't actually seen a man's. . . a penis before.'

'It took you more than a year before you would look again.'

'You're lucky I *ever* looked again.'

They stood in the grassy fields where twenty-three years earlier they'd made tentative pre-sexual love. If his mother or her mother were not at home they would sometimes go there and pet more until they ached and were almost sick from arousal without release.

As they stood there in the long grass, she said, 'I sometimes wonder what gave me the cancer, was it – this is silly I know but I have to say it – could it have been men's penises not being clean enough?'

He tried to joke. 'I don't think so – British women would all have cervical cancer.' It was a typical idea for her to have, and, who knows, maybe right.

'I don't mean you,' she touched him, 'you were a good middle-class boy and clean, but well, others. . .' She gave a small guarding smile as if he might even now be upset by mention of other men, 'others after you weren't always good middle-class boys.'

'Did a doctor suggest this?'

'No, it's a private theory, I have lots of private theories these days. Being ill in a serious way gives you a special sense of knowing your body.'

They left the school. 'I always remember the Head saying something that was very important to me,' she said, 'remember him saying that school wasn't preparation for life – it was real life, real living. It's true, and school is an important part of living.'

In the car she suggested she'd like to go to the church where they'd been married.

Outside the church he said how normal their lives had looked then – church, fellowship, Sunday School, confirmation, débutantes, engagements, balls, marriages, births.

'I missed out on confirmation,' he said to her, 'that was one of my protests.'

'But you *were* confirmed,' she said, 'I was the one who refused to be confirmed and caused all the ruckus.'

'No,' he said, feeling determinedly sure, 'I was the one who refused to be confirmed.'

'No, sorry, I was the one who held out, you were forced into it by your mother but you were certainly confirmed.'

He flushed, she was right, he'd been rewriting his history. Why? When had he started that legend – lie – and then forgotten to correct it?

'You talked about doing it,' she said, 'you talked of rebellion but your mother put great pressure on you. My mother oddly enough was a bit against it for some reason. Low church – found it too popish.'

He was embarrassed, he must have made up the story when he was a teenager in Sydney as part of the picture of rebellious adolescence in a country town.

'Are you honestly confused?' she asked.

'What does it matter now,' he said, 'yes, you were the one.'

They went into the dim church and walked up the aisle where they'd walked as nineteen-year-old bride and groom. 'Is this the altar?' he asked her. 'I never quite knew where the altar began.'

'Yes, but Rev. Benson called it the communion table.'

'The altar was where they once sacrificed animals.'

'Not in this old town,' she said, 'here we sacrificed kids. Kids like us.'

She turned to him then with tears and came to him. 'Hold me.'

She held on to him.

'It's OK,' he said, 'you're OK, Robyn.'

'I'm dying,' she said, 'I know it.'

'You're fighting it – you'll win, you were always a winner.'

'We will at least know all the answers then,' she said.

Towards what end?

She looked up at him hopelessly. 'Marry me again – just for today – let's marry for the day. We may never see each other again anyhow, whatever happens.'

He strove to get her meaning.

By 'marry' he assumed she meant they should pledge to each other some vow of affection.

'We were little children together,' she said, 'and we went through all that stuff of adolescence, and we were each other's first love, and I did bear your child – even if you never claimed her.'

He had lived as if this child did not exist. He had decided years back that he could not be a father for the child because of the circumstances, his alienation from Robyn, his emotional deficiency. But he'd also made the decision to protect himself from the pain of being held away from the child. If he had once permitted his fatherly feelings free rein they would have tormented him forever. He had still to keep them unreleased. He had explained this to Robyn on a number of occasions but she had never accepted it. He wouldn't try again.

He knew then for the first time, or faced for the first time, the fact that parenthood had passed him by.

He'd passed through another of the doorways.

He felt no deep affection for her. He felt a sympathetic bond of, probably, a unique kind. He didn't feel caught up in a rush of new affection or restored affections. Perhaps he felt sentimental. What he felt most was recoil from her disease. This continued to make him angry with himself.

'You do still feel something for me?' she asked.

'Yes, a lot.'

'Do you feel some love for me?'

'Of course I do,' he lied, softly, searching for some validation of this in whatever fudged and twisted way, yes, there was a unique place for her in his personal history. 'Yes, you are in a special place in my heart.'

Why not lie? He was frightened that a lie would be detected by the antennae of her unconscious and hurt her more.

'Do you take me,' she whispered, 'as your spiritual wife for this day and for all days until we die, from this day forth?'

All he could react to was her extension of the make-believe vows from one day to 'until death'. She was taking pleasure from the pseudo-ecclesiastical wording of it too.

'Yes.'

'No,' she said with insistence, 'say it to me, say the words.'

'I take you as my spiritual wife for this day.' He wanted to conclude it there.

'. . .and for all days until I die, from this day forth,' she instructed him.

At first he noted that she changed the wording to refer to her death, but when he said it, it made it *his* death, '. . .and for all the days until I die, from this day forth.'

'Now ask me.'

He was acutely uncomfortable, worried that someone might come into the church and come across them doing this.

'Come on,' she said, sensing his reluctance, 'do it for me.'

'Do you take me as your spiritual husband for this day and for all days until I die, from this day forth?'

'Yes, yes I take you, Ian, as my spiritual husband for this day and for all days until I die, from this day forth.' she said with a forceful sincerity.

'You may now kiss the bride,' she said, smiling, and he was ashamed that he could not give himself to the kiss with a wholehearted spirit, instead he changed the kiss into a brotherly kiss but it was enough of a personal kiss for her to believe it to be, for it to suit the prescribed kind of love and the vows of the occasion. He sincerely hoped she would accept it as the kiss she wanted.

Maybe if he'd been able to give her that kiss passionately without withholding, maybe if he had been able to make love to her on that visit to the home town - or at least give her physical embraces of a wholehearted kind - she would have stayed alive. Maybe with her method those gestures by him would have been enough to tip the balance. Maybe she died because of people like him in the world. Maybe he was a negative cell. Or maybe this was egocentric thinking and placed him unrealistically large and unrealistically close in her personal galaxy.

He was in the bar at the UN City in Vienna, drinking alone, when he heard of her death from Mark Madden, an American chemist with the NEA who had been her lover at some time after the marriage.

Madden and he also had been close for a few months when he'd come to Australia as a young student drop-out. They'd re-met on the IAEA circuit at times. Despite these close links and their respective distances from their homelands, he and Madden now usually avoided each other in the bar. This night Madden had come across to him and said, 'Robyn died this morning, I thought you mightn't have heard.'

Why would Madden think that? But yes, Madden was right, he hadn't heard.

'God,' he said, 'that's rotten.'

He felt a real sadness and a regret for her now permanent absence from his life, or to be precise, the 'absent presence' she'd been in his life since they'd separated.

'She was a sweet, sweet person, a very special sort of human being,' Madden said, as they had a drink together. That sort of talk, he thought, was why he didn't drink with Madden.

'I knew her as a giggling hockey-playing schoolgirl,' he said to Madden, 'that is my enduring memory.' It was a way of asserting the superiority of his knowing of her over Madden's knowing of her. Two male egos still clashing like stags over her dead body.

'She was essentially a poetic person.'

'Poetic? I never saw her as poetic. I didn't see that side of her.' Nor did he believe it.

'It wasn't a "side of her" it was the whole damned person.'

'I'm not doubting you Mark, just that I knew a much different Robyn. How do you mean poetic anyhow?'

'I mean, man, that she wrote poetry.'

He and Madden had once been really close and now it was nearly all animal antipathy.

'Robyn wrote poetry?'

'She had poems in magazines. Yes.'

He was surprised by this and resented Madden knowing and his not knowing.

Privately he still felt his relationship to Robyn to be superior to whatever she'd had with Madden, but he was finding it impossibly disorienting to believe that this self-important, unnaturally fit, tomato-juice-drinking chemist in the tartan check trousers and black jacket could have been a lover of a girl he had once been married to and shared innocence with. He noted alcoholically that he was now released from his secret vow to her in the home-town church. Not that the vow had carried any obligations but it had from time to time invaded his consciousness in an ill-defined way, suggesting obligations which he could not discover.

Nor could he match this guy Madden with the guitar-playing gentle American youth he'd known in those years before. It seemed wasteful of nature to have put all that growing into that guitar-playing youth only for it to come out as the NEA chemist, Madden.

'When was it that you had an affair with her?' He thought he might as well drop niceties and delve into matters he'd always left unexamined. Or maybe it was information he'd once had and which his mind had not held.

'Robyn and I did not have an "affair".'

'I didn't mean to demean it.'

He did wish to demean it.

'As you know, it was after you two had split. I had two periods of loving Robyn - in New York years ago, in the old peace movement days with SANE and then again much later in Lisbon, when she was stringing for the *Herald-Tribune*. We were very close then in Lisbon.'

We-were-very-close-then-in-Lisbon.

'And I became very fond of your daughter Chris.'

'She hardly qualifies as my daughter.'

'Hell man - face up to yourself - she's your daughter. She's living with some guy old enough to be her father - if you're in anyways interested - out in the mid-west somewhere.'

'Robyn said she was OK.' He didn't want to know about the child. People shouldn't tell him about the child. He could not afford to know about the child.

'Hell she is.'

They sat there in their own silences.

He tried to remain sociable. He had no bond with his biological daughter. They'd had nothing to do with each other since her birth. He maybe would come to regret this but now he felt nothing for her state, no inclination to try to make a bond with her. Impossible. Would she come seeking her 'real' father one day and go away bewildered and disappointed that he was not a mythical father but simply a crumbling, solitary international civil servant who'd failed to become a writer, who drank too much? A man of too little feeling. That wasn't true. He wept weekly. But for what did he weep? He was perhaps, though, someone who did not know how to live properly, he would tell her.

'I told her to try everything - she said she'd given up chemotherapy. I told her to have conventional therapy and alternative therapy at the same time.'

'That was bad advice, friend. She wanted faith not smartarsed advice. The last thing she needed was to be steered back to invasive therapy.'

He should have known that Madden would be that sort of person. He did hope though that he had strengthened Robyn's will. Or was that wrong? Should he have instead argued more strongly against the hocus-pocus? Maybe that was his true offence against her. Not challenging her irrationality strongly enough.

Madden went on, 'She had to go for it, health and disease, the whole caboodle. Wasn't it Mann who said that disease is simply love transformed? She had to turn the disease back into love.'

'I thought that maybe self-help was the disease disguised. Disease disguised as therapy. Neurosis pretending to be the doctor.'

'She was trying self-love - I don't see that as disease.'

'Well we know now she was either on the wrong therapy or she didn't have enough self-love.'

'Or she began too late after being screwed about with Cobalt 60.'

'I thought you were a man of science.'

'I am a scientist and that's why I'm open to new strategies. I know we don't know it all, Sean.'

Madden was one of the few people in his life who still called him Sean. A leftover part of their former intimacy. Madden had forgotten that Sean was not the name he went by.

'Did you encourage her to try the other therapies?'

'Yes, I did. I put her onto the Simonton technique.'

'You filled her full of crap, in other words.'

'Don't call it crap when you know fuck-all about it.'

'It is crap and she's dead to prove it.'

Alcohol was making him reckless.

'I take strong exception to that remark.'

'Do what you bloody well like with it.'

Again they lapsed into their own silences, but both with increased pulse rates and broken breathing.

He then recalled something from his marriage and felt sickened by the recall. He had not thought about it since that time. It had not come to him during their reunion in the home town.

It was in the collapsing days of the marriage, or just before when they had been trying to restore its zest. Or maybe he'd really given up and hadn't cared what happened. He'd intimidated or inveigled her into sexual games, including an episode with a whip. Now that he looked back on it, knowing also more about himself, he had wanted to be the whipped one but had in fact whipped her. She'd gone along with it all and responded to it as sex play, but it hadn't helped the relationship. Probably because they'd got it back to front – that is, if she really had any such inclinations residing in her personality and had wanted to whip him. She was happier though with things closer to the orthodox. He wasn't sure how much the games had been created out of frustration, rage, about their blocked and dulled relationship. But the thought which pushed itself into his mind now there in the UN bar in Vienna was a remark she'd made after one of those nights. She'd said apologetically that she wished she were 'better at it', but that she'd been frightened of being whipped on the breasts because she feared that it could give her cancer. He'd denied this possibility – on no knowledge whatsoever. He now knew that a blow can cause cancer. Not that they'd been exchanging 'blows' or really striking each other with any force. At the time he'd laughed at her for equating sexual deviance with sickness and cancer as the punishment for dabbling in evil. He wished he'd sought her forgiveness about this before she died.

'God I loved that woman,' Madden said, with an even more emphatic American sincerity, fuelled probably by the tequila that he was now drinking, having switched from tomato juice. Having drunk down the tequila and ordered another immediately, as if the speed of his drinking publicly proved his grief. Then he said, 'And she was damned bright – one of the brightest women I've met.' This was said in an affirmative way, as if Madden was 'pulling' himself up out of the grief.

He wished Madden would piss off and leave him free to dwell on her death in his own maudlin way. And he didn't want to be in the UN bar. It was too brightly lit, too much a bar of publicly acceptable behaviour, a bar to be in after work not after after-work. Madden was the wrong person to be with.

'Oh come on, Madden, she was many good things but she wasn't bright in that sense. She was a very good journalist but she was not intellectual. At times I found her painfully banal.'

'You callous bastard – I ought to sock you.'

Sock you. High school language.

Sock you.

He wouldn't mind a fist fight with Madden there in the 'school' bar. Turbulence and disorder would discharge his frustrated urge to be maudlin.

But no, the institutionalised setting had them both in its command.

He stood up, grunted a goodbye to Madden, put down a pocketful of schillings and left to go back into Vienna. To an old bar. To the grand bar of the Imperial where he might be grandly maudlin. As he walked out in the night air to the train station he said to Robyn out there in the cosmos, 'You were a bright burning flame of a girl Robyn, and you were for a time my passion, but oh why did you go with guys like Madden?'

Or guys like him. But she hadn't gone with him when he was a 'guy', she had gone with him when he was a boy.

The train took him across the Danube.

He had another thought: 'She went with guys like Madden therefore I am a guy like Madden.'

Ah, the time of self-laceration. If he couldn't be maudlin he could be self-lacerating.

No, she would have not been involved with him if she'd met him as an adult. Or would she? What was the difference between Madden and him – both solitary men adrift in an international community? Community?

He'd had great personal power as a youth in that small town, a student prince in his imitation of flamboyance, his curious, neurotic energy. Now he was something of a drunk, a failed writer, a 'co-ordinator' of reports.

At the first drink in the Imperial he observed that he was not a 'guy like Madden'. He was a guy who could perceive the possibility that he was a guy like Madden and fear it. He was therefore not a guy like Madden. Madden was not sitting in the UN bar fearing that he was like him. Madden had no doubts about his nature.

Sometime during the evening, back at his hotel, he tried to call his lost girlfriend in London but a rough male street-voice, maybe West Indian, answered and hung up. That relationship was hopelessly corrupted by fantasy and beyond his comprehension for the time. He rang Belle back in Australia but she was not able to participate in his maudlin mourning for his ex-wife and suggested that he should go to sleep.

He went back to bed wishing that he had never known his ex-wife, only his wife. No. He wished he'd known only the hockey-playing girl who was to become his wife.

• RAMBLING BOY •

He came over to me, parting the bushes of the party to reach me.

'I met your wife,' he said. 'I met her in New York with SANE.'

His American voice was like fingertips on my face. But my wife. Robyn. My wife? Why did the word still pinch me? Now. She was not my wife except in law but perhaps it was the alcohol and perhaps I am sick and perhaps Lawrence was right and she will for always be my wife. For another man she can be only his woman. Even if she married she would not be his first wife nor his first love. What's intrinsically inferior about second?

'. . .after a committee meeting.'

'I'm sorry. I wasn't listening. You met Robyn. And how is she? And Chris, my little girl, did you see her?'

'My holy God - the noise of these parties and what–all. No, I didn't see your little girl. I met Robyn after a SANE committee meeting. She's fine. She's a lovable person. I know that you don't communicate, but she said to look you up.'

'Oh.'

'I'm Mark. Mark Madden. I'm a bum.'

'What sort of a bum?'

'The worst sort - a folk-singing bum. I'm afraid I'm not singing for anything tonight. I'm eating and drinking but not singing a note - freeloading.'

'You'll sing some other time. Have a drink. Drink is communal. In theory, anyhow.'

'Have a drink! That's all you Aussies ever say. These parties! I've got to hand it to you - you fellows can drink.'

I watched his face and heard his voice.

'Have you a place to live?'

'No, not as yet.'

'Stay with me.'

He had a sleeping bag and he slept in that on a settee and I lay in my own double bed. A bed which I was aware was half-empty even when a girl stayed there for a stray hungry night. I wormed naked into the warm zone of the bed and thought of Mark. I had liked his eyes and his voice and his words. Now I thought of his body. And then I wondered about what was happening to me. I put my cheek against a thought which I have never touched. And I slept.

'I feel lost from the world, Sean. I am a wanderer. I am a singer of other people's songs. I walk in other people's lands. I usually sleep in other people's beds. There's no me. There's only other people.'

'But what about Oregon and your home?'

'It's ten years since I was there. For godsake it was never home. It was a man called my father and some woman called my mother. And shit-house brawls. I left as soon as I could walk alone after dark. I was afraid of going but I was afraid to stay. I'm afraid now. But Jesus, we are all afraid.'

We looked at our beers and I thought about being afraid. I was more afraid at times when I cared about things and events. I felt afraid now of a *feeling*. And I remembered the things I was afraid of now and then when I cared and I said: 'There's a lot to be afraid of. Political things like bombs and being forced to go to war and psychological things like fucked-up sex and being crippled with things like cancer and car accidents. There's neurotic unreality - a thing that can happen to you and you don't realise it until you fall down somewhere and are dragged away screaming.'

'You know, Sean, you feel the world the way I feel the world. But I take no risk and no responsibility. At least you take risks - your marriage and your child was a risk - at least you took it. God knows I've never tried. Peace and war. At least you speak on the public platform as a chemist. All I've done was to go to one meeting of the Banners sub-committee – and then only because of some girl. So I sing a few protest songs in some out-of-the-way coffee shops. But that's just by drift – not by decision. Drift and drift. That's me.'

'We all drift most of the time. I try now and then, I suppose I try.'

There in the alcove of the pub our hands gripped. Mine partly the grip of a mate and partly the grip of a lover. Mark's? How did Mark's hand grip? And then a blush. And then a laugh. And another beer so that we could go normally on. Why did we hold to grim normality?

'My Jesus! This harbour – and these ferries. They're wild. This mid-morning fog and the city, a ghost over there, grey and the ships, ghosts, grey. I'm moved by it, Sean.'

'People who work on boats are different in the way they work – temperament. They talk to people as if they are people. They're not eroded and suspicious and hostile. These people are refreshed by the sea.'

'I believe it.'

'Play something.'

'I suppose no one would mind. There's hardly anyone on the damn ferry.'

The certain strumming. The tuning. The listening ear. The tuning fingers.

So here's to you, my rambling boy.
May all your rambling bring you joy.
So here's to you my rambling boy.

Some people make you see the world. They make buildings and streets and manhole covers reach out their actuality. The water and the sky touch you. And your footsteps are each important and your breathing.

We heard Beethoven played in the dark as we lay on the carpet and looked through the window at the dark harbour, spotted by moving lights, on a spring night. I wanted to touch him but there are ten miles between two men. And there was Louise he was sleeping with now and then, and there was Cindy I said I loved and who I knew would come back to me one day. I cried then. Hoping he'd hear.

'Why do you cry?'

'The music. Wine and my life and its mess and its good times. And for you. And being twenty-nine and the way more dense and confused.'

I felt the music joined us and I was touching him through it.

'Why do you cry for me?'

'You mean something to me. You're a close mate.' Meaning I feel love for you.

'We're close. We're mates and it's good.'

But do you feel love, Mark? You once said I feel the world the way you feel the world. Do you feel me the way I feel you?

'Do you remember Mark, the time we gripped each other's hand?'

'Yes, I do. I remember.'

'I was thinking then about that.'

I looked to the back of his neck and his long proud hair and wanted to reach and touch him, but I couldn't.

'I shouldn't but I am.'

'Why?'

'Because I'm a restless cunt. I'm a bum. I've always been restless. I know I won't find peace or whatever it is, if I stay. I can find it only for a time. It has always been like this.'

'But we've found a pretty good time.'

'But it will go if I stay. I want to go before it goes.'

'How do you know it will go?'

'I know. Because all situations destroy themselves. I know.'

'Will you come back?'

'Yes. That will be a new situation, then.'

'Where will you go?'

'I'll go back through Oregon for God knows what reason. And I'll go to Alaska where I haven't been. Out of this summer into cool snow.'

'What do you want, Mark?'

'I don't know. I really don't know. I don't know if I'm searching or avoiding. Kids? A wife who will understand me and bear with my restlessness or dispel it? An end to being restless? Or to be always restless?'

'Play – play something.'

He touched the strings. He smiled at me.

So here's to you, my rambling boy.
May all your rambles bring you joy.

'Remember you played that on the ferry that foggy morning?'
'I remember, Sean, I remember everything we've done.'
He sang the song about himself because I couldn't sing it to him.
And I felt tight because I could never touch him.

That quay was blown with wind. It had wheat spilled its splintering
length. It had fifteen lights, each not reaching far into the resisting
night. At the end of the fifteen lights lay a German tramp steamer
with a name I could not pronounce and have not remembered. Mark
had his duffle bag and wore his duffle coat. I walked with my hands
in my pockets.
'It's a tub.'
'It'll probably go no further than the Heads and there sink forever.'
'No union rates on this.'
No one else was on the dark quay. A long emptiness.
'Well, *bon voyage*, Mark. That's what's to be said, isn't it?'
His hand on my arm. That was allowed.
'They've been sweet months, Sean, sweet, sweet months. Four
sweet seasons. I don't know what else can be said.'
'That's enough. Four sweet seasons.'

• CAVES •

During the year 1911 Jenolan was visited by 8460 persons who paid 21 325 visits of inspection to the various caves. – Percy Hunter, Superintendent, Immigration and Tourist Bureau.

The statistics for the Jenolan limestone caves of New South Wales included more than bona fide visitors, they included his great-grandmother's visits to the Caves as a whore.

The police documents described his great-grandmother's methods when she first worked as a young whore from Blackheath, Katoomba, and the caves in the Blue Mountains. She would join a party of men and go with them to the Jenolan Caves where she would stay overnight at the guest house, sharing herself among the men.

Earlier in her career she used to attract the attention of male parties while they had a pint for the road or whatever at the Carrington, the Ivanhoe, the Hydroa, or the Hydro Majestic. They would suggest to her that she join them for a lark, a jaunt down to the Caves. Later she worked from the Caves guest house.

According to the evidence, earlier in her career she pretended not to have been to the Caves and usually implied that she would lose wages if she went to the Caves with them.

The men would offer to make up her wages and she would accept. At some point she dropped this pretence.

He stood in the room at the Hydro Majestic, in the disused wing, at the room number given as one of her addresses during that time. The room was fairly much as it had been in her day. It might have been painted, but the fittings were from the turn of the century. The Hydro had had its own electric generator quite early but the electrical switches and fittings were dated. It was no longer part of the Hydro offered to the public as accommodation.

If she lived today, he thought, she would have advertised in the Katoomba newspaper as Trixie, Delilah or Monique and offered 'relaxing massage', advertised 'motel visits'.

He touched the chipped 'Dreadnought' enamel hand basin, cold water only. She must have used the basin for her ablutions. The room belonged back with the days of rail, spas, health resorts.

'You say your grandmother lived in this room once?'

'Yes, great-grandmother,' he said to the manager, who had been persuaded to rent him the room.

'As long as you're happy, as you can see it's not up to scratch.'

'No, it's OK. It's how I thought it would be. It's a nostalgia trip.'

'I had them sweep it out but there wasn't much more we could do with it.'

'It's OK.'

He dropped his luggage and took off his coat and with this the manager left him.

He sat on the bed. The bed. He took out the First World War hip flask which had come down to him from his great-grandmother and drank deeply from the cognac. He'd fantasised that the flask belonged to a young lover of hers. It was certainly not what would have been considered a woman's flask. He saw men offering her drinks from their flasks, seeing it as a test of her attitude to life, she knowing this, swigging from it with gusto, letting them know what sort of woman she was prepared to be for them. But somehow she'd ended up with a flask in her possession. Now in his possession.

He opened the drawers, papered with newspapers about forty years old, not as he'd hoped eighty years old. They were her drawers though, she'd opened them, put her lace, silk and satin into them.

The electric light globe was only 25 watts and the dimness pleased him, it was more the strength of light of her times.

In the village of Blackheath he stood at the war memorial and wondered how many of the names on the list of dead had visited her before they went to Gallipoli, the Somme, the Sinai. Maybe they had talked about doing it but never got around to it before they left.

That she'd been stunningly beautiful might have daunted some of the younger ones. She had left 144 photographs of herself posing with men at the Caves – posing at the Devil's Canyon or the Grand Arch. Many were almost identical photographs and he had at first mistaken them for copies. He'd then noticed that the faces of the men were different from photograph to photograph.

The staff at the Caves must have known her. How did she prevent them making snide remarks about her changing male companionship? Maybe she paid them. She had eventually stopped pretending and for a time lived at the Caves guest house where it must have been accepted.

Going to the River Caves, the Temple of Baal, the Skeleton Cave, the Left Imperial, the Right Imperial, acting out exclamations of pleasure each of those 144 times.

He'd day-dreamed about the Caves and Katoomba and the Hydro Majestic while he'd been in Europe. He'd dreamed of the dim limestone caves and the grand hotels of Katoomba's grand days, the distinguished guest houses. He'd wanted to live among the relics and possessions of those times, he'd wanted to buy back his great-grandmother's guest house, restock the library with short-story collections, *Punch* magazine, *London Illustrated News*, the old *Bulletin*. He'd wanted to go alone into the huge limestone caves at Jenolan and be quiet and alone.

He and Belle had prowled the guest house, brothel, home of his great-grandmother. The place was dilapidated.

He wanted to insinuate himself into the intimacy of another generation and another time. He wanted to live among the obsolete and the quaint. To go away from his times, not because he disliked his times, but because of some genetic calling.

'I became what I became deliberately and with as much good grace and pleasure as I could find,' she'd written at twenty. He wondered how deliberate it really had been.

Her travelling rug, her travelling drinking cups and the officer's hip flask had come down to him. But hardly anything written by her. He held the rug to his face, trying to inhale the essence. There had been the photographs and a piece of a stalactite. He ran his finger over a stain on the rug, smelled it again, willing it to be the stain of his great-grandmother.

Standing in the River Cave he shivered as he fingered the piece of stalactite. It had probably been broken off by one of the men who'd taken her there. How many pieces of limestone did men break off for her? She'd kept only one piece. They'd had to close the Arch Cave from which it probably came because too many pieces had been broken off in the early days. A 'Goth' from Bathurst had destroyed five columns one day.

He stood there now in the Caves wanting to replace the one piece, but as the guide boomed with false animation he decided that it would be foolish to leave it. And he could not bear to part with it.

'The Arch Cave, now closed, is separated from the Nettle Cave underneath by a thin layer of rock. You can hear footsteps above you. The Belfry at the end will give out musical sounds when struck and can be heard as far away as the Imperial Cave.'

The Caves were repairing themselves. He kept the piece.

In the Sculptor's Studio he saw 'the unfinished statues and grotesque forms'. The likeness of a woman with a large bonnet. The bird and animal in combat. The giant mushroom. The hands of Joshua. The Lobster. The Judge's Wig. The Orator with a bald forehead and white locks down to his shoulders, one arm raised.

The guide explained that the Mons Meg formation was named after a cannon standing outside Edinburgh Castle.

Had she spent the night with one man after she'd shared her favours among them?

One day last year he'd entered a Sydney antique shop and found no one at the counter. Signs were everywhere explaining method of payment, information about the items. He rang the bell and a woman appeared from the back of the shop.

In the low light the woman appeared to be hiding herself, the way she held her head down. He realised that it was a girl he'd known years earlier who'd been a whore. He was about to say to her, 'Don't we know each other?' but stopped, realising that she'd seen too many faces in her life to be likely to remember him.

She'd told him what he'd wanted to know about the inkpot and then returned to the back of the shop.

Afterwards he'd thought that maybe all the signs in the shop were to avoid questions and limit customer contact.

The Caves' guide called the stalactites 'decorations' and talked of 'nature the silent artist'.

'We look to find the truth,' the guide said, 'but find mystery.' He looked for traces.

He saw Victorian sexuality embalmed here, of both sexes, of all the sexual fluids. He saw the Caves through the eyes of his great-grandmother because they remained as they were when she'd lived, and when she'd come there.

The Charon, the Confectioner's Shop, the River Styx. The Enchanted Forest. The Devil's Table.

He went back to his room at the Hydro Majestic. He had to go to Canberra for a service to mark the death of his friend Edith and report to the office. His contract had not yet been renewed.

He drank. He lay on the bed, looked again and again at the few remnants of her life, fondled the piece of stalactite. He took 'scenic walks' but most were now overgrown.

He extended his stay at the hotel for another month despite the spareness of the room and the manager gave up pestering him with offers of a better room.

He prowled the old guest houses, visited antique shops, visited the tourist 'attractions' of her time, now unvisited and run down. He had fantasies of buying her old guest house. Or he thought of working in the Caves as a guide and telling better stories to the visitors to the Caves. He would tell them different, more elaborate stories, he would rename the Caves, weave in the story of his great-grandmother's life. His life. He would change the commentary slightly every day until it was totally his.

After his visits to the surrounding villages and to Katoomba he would come back to his room having bought something she might have had in her life, a hair brush, a nail-care set, a perfume bottle.

The room began to fill with the shapes and objects of her life.

He received a note from his office in Canberra saying that his contract would not be renewed.

He was now living entirely on her – the wealth he'd inherited from her.

He liked it.

One day he came home with some dresses and a corset from her times and he knew then that he was falling down a genetic spiral. He didn't mind.

• THE THIRD POST CARD •

His young girlfriend in London wrote him a third post card.
She addressed it to him at the Hydro Majestic Hotel where he was
staying, where he and Belle used to stay, in the depressed, run-down,
turn-of-the-century health resort district around Katoomba where his
great-grandmother used to operate.

The postcard said:

If I offered you £100 would you consider us getting together in Vienna,
London, or at this weird address where you're living in the mountains? Why
are you living there? Are you writing that book at last? The Durruti story is
really great. But you and I know the 'full story'. Let's get together and talk
about a love formed from the discipline of indiscipline. And don't you think
it's time I stopped whoring and you became a father? You once said we had
become footnotes to a poem by Levine. Isn't it time the footnotes became
their own story?